Tales of the Were
Lick of Fire 2

Phoenix and the Wolf

BIANCA D'ARC

This book is a work of fiction. The names, characters, places, and incidents are products of the writer's imagination or have been used fictitiously and are not to be construed as real. Any resemblance to persons, living or dead, actual events, locale or organizations is entirely coincidental.

No part of this book may be used or reproduced in any manner whatsoever without written permission, except in the case of brief quotations embodied in critical articles and reviews.

AUTHOR'S NOTE
& DEDICATION

Note: The phoenix trilogy is an offshoot of my *Tales of the Were* series, which has many nooks and crannies. This set fits after the *Redstone Clan* and overlaps a bit with the latter part of *Grizzly Cove* and the *Grizzly Cove Crossroads* set. The phoenix books (there will be three of them) can be read as a standalone set or in conjunction with any of my other paranormals, since they all take place in the same basic world, just in different parts of it. Characters do crossover and make cameo appearances from time to time. For a complete rundown of all my books check the list at the end of this book or you can always check my website – BIANCADARC.COM - which will always have the most up-to-date book list.

I'd like to dedicate this book to Oma,

who I lost more than three decades ago. I would've liked to have had more time with her to get to know her as an adult and learn from her wisdom. I'm not one for lots of photos, but I keep a photo of her on my desk, right next to my computer screen, along with a series of snapshots of my mother and I, when I was little. I have a few of my dad as well, but that's it. Oma was a big influence on my life, even though I only knew her for a short time.

I'd also like to send special thanks to my editor, Jess, who fit this edit in right before she went on vacation. Now that's dedication! Thanks, Jess, for the quick turnaround, and I promise to do better on timing with the next one.

PROLOGUE

Diana felt the stirring of flame beneath her skin. Again. Something was calling to her. Something out in the desert. Something she didn't understand and was afraid to acknowledge.

She had dabbled in Wicca as a teen, but the power that rose inside her now scared her. She was an adult and had put lucky charms and love potions behind her. So, why did she feel this strange calling to go out to the desert and...fly?

It just didn't make sense, but something had changed in recent days. Some power had awoken and was causing a reaction down deep in her psyche—in her soul. It was as if she was finally waking up after a long sleep, though why she felt that way, she had no idea.

Diana needed answers, but she didn't quite know how to go about getting them. She only knew that, somewhere out on the edge of town, she might find a clue. Now, the real question was, did she dare go after it?

CHAPTER ONE

Oma was having a good day, which meant Diana could go out and do some grocery shopping, leaving her grandmother on her own for a bit. She wasn't completely alone, of course. Currently, Diana's oma—the Dutch word meaning grandma—was having tea and cookies with her next-door neighbor. Oma had learned how to text recently and was sending images through of the petit fours and the pretty teapot her neighbor had chosen for the occasion.

Mrs. Peabody had emigrated from the United Kingdom about sixty years ago as a young bride, but she'd never left her British roots behind. Tea and cakes were served promptly at four each afternoon, and more often than not, Oma went over to join her friend for the occasion. Diana thought Oma was probably doing it so that Diana could leave and not worry about her grandmother being alone in the condo, but they never spoke of it.

Either way, if Diana had something that needed doing, she'd usually arrange it for the late afternoon. It was her "me" time. It was an hour or so, away from the needs of her sole remaining family member, the grandmother who meant the world to Diana, and who encouraged her to go out and meet people her own age whenever possible.

They both knew Diana's social life had been harshly curtailed by the need to be with her oma. Again, that was something they seldom spoke of, though Diana was well aware that her grandmother worried Diana would never meet her mate stuck in a condo all day with an old woman. Diana didn't see a solution. Not without something drastic happening… And she certainly didn't want that.

Oma was all she had left in the world. The only link to her past. To her family And, since Diana's mother and uncle—Oma's only children—were both gone, Diana was the only family Oma had left, too.

Diana dreaded the day that Oma would leave her. Diana didn't know what she'd do when that happened, but she'd have to move for a start. The condo community they lived in was for those aged fifty-five and over. When Oma died, Diana would have to move out, and she had no idea where to go.

Grim thoughts.

Diana shook them away and tried to concentrate on the here and now. She had errands to run, and they weren't going to take care of themselves while she let anxiety run rampant through her brain.

Just as she had that thought, the engine of her old SUV sputtered. Sputtered…then died. *Shit.*

She reached into her purse for her cell phone, only to find the battery was dead. The old thing was holding a charge for shorter and shorter periods, but she hadn't had time to get anything fixed. Her schedule was too full just trying to keep her grandmother going from day to day. Diana never had any time for herself lately. Not even enough time to go to the store and figure out if she needed a new battery or an entirely new phone. Darn it.

She looked around and realized she was on the outskirts of town, in an industrial area. She scanned the signs over the nearest businesses on the same side of the street. No help there unless she wanted a vacuum repaired or a new air conditioning unit. She turned to look at the other side of the street, and a chill went down her spine, despite the non-functional air system in her car. She was directly across the street from an auto repair shop.

At least, that's what the sign that hung over the top of a metal gate said. She could see lots of cars inside the lot, and a few people in the distance. Though she'd never noticed this repair shop before, it looked like it was a big place that did a lot of business. She grabbed her purse and got out of her SUV, crossing the street and ducking into the yard.

She stopped short. First, the caliber of automobile in here was much higher than the domestic SUV she'd bought used a few years ago. Could she even afford to have this shop look at her car? She looked around again, recognizing the luxury names of sports cars she'd never even seen in person before.

Yeah. She probably couldn't afford this place. But maybe she could use their phone, at least.

The other reason she'd stopped in the entrance to the yard was the weird vibe coming from the place. She couldn't quite place what was different, but something definitely had her spidey senses tingling. Or, maybe, it was just the six-figure cars intimidating her as they sat silent, awaiting attention, all over the place. Judging her and her old beater of an SUV.

"Don't be ridiculous," she counseled herself as she made her foot cross the threshold. "Cars don't judge people."

"You might be surprised." The low, almost growly, amused voice came from her left, and Diana whipped around, one hand raised in fright.

She wasn't sure what she planned to do with that raised hand. It was clear from one glance at the behemoth walking toward her from the left of the entrance that she would be no match for this guy. None at all. Not even after the five karate lessons her friend had given her as a twentieth birthday gift, hoping she might like it and stay in the class.

She'd felt clumsy and totally uncoordinated, so she hadn't gone back after the gift sessions were up. Her friend had been a black belt, of course, and sort of glided in his uber-coordinated way. Not like a normal human being at all. Almost like this guy who was walking toward her. Or, rather, *prowling* toward her. There was no other word to describe the almost predatory slink of this man's slim hips.

Hubba hubba.

"You okay, miss?" Yes, he was definitely laughing at her, now. She must look like a landed fish, her mouth gaping open while her brain seemed to wander onto all sorts of tangents.

"My car..." she managed, making a vague gesture toward the road. *Good one, Diana. Let the guy think you're a complete moron.*

He looked out the wide entrance of the yard toward her old SUV parked across the street. His expression wasn't judgmental, for which she was thankful. No, if anything, she'd say he looked intrigued.

8

"Want me to take a look?" His stunning brown eyes came back to rest on her, and she tried not to fidget. Had she ever talked to a more handsome specimen of manhood? Diana thought not.

"I'm not sure I can afford this place," she said hesitantly, gesturing toward the expensive car he'd apparently just parked to the left of the entrance. It was shiny and new and looked like it probably cost more than she made in a year...or maybe a decade. "I thought maybe I could just use your phone..." She let her sentence trail off when he started shaking his head.

"Never let it be said I turned away a damsel in distress." With that, he started walking across the street.

The man had a power about him. A vibe. Like coiled energy. He was intimidating, in a way, but it didn't really bother her. Diana wasn't a mouse. Not by a long shot. In fact, most people found her a bit too forceful. Make that, most *men* found her too forceful. The guys she'd dated had complained that she was too independent and she didn't let them take care of her enough.

What a load of crap. Maybe she just needed to find a man who was more secure in his own masculinity than the saps she'd been dating, darn it. That's what she preferred to believe, because there was no way she would become a simpering helpless female to suit anyone.

And, once again, she was woolgathering while the hunky guy in the ripped jeans jogged across the road and lifted the hood on her ancient clunker. He took a moment to check a few things then raised his head and let out a sharp, short whistle, his head turned in the direction of the open gate of the car lot. She hadn't even made it across the road, yet. Too busy oogling the sexy mechanic.

She wondered how he thought anybody could hear his short whistle from all the way across the road. She'd barely heard it, and she'd been looking right at him. Curious, she turned her head to find at least a half-dozen men raise their heads from under car hoods or out of car doors all around the giant yard. They'd heard him?

Eyes wide with surprise, she turned back in time to see the guy by her car raise one hand with four fingers then make the universal *come here* gesture. He turned back to the engine, as if certain his hand signals

10

would be not only seen, but obeyed.

Sure enough, a moment later, four of the guys who'd been secreted about the yard doing other work jogged past her. The last one in line paused by her side for a moment, holding out one hand.

"Keys?" he asked with a winning smile.

Diana found herself depositing her lucky keychain in the young man's hand and shaking her head in wonder. These guys must have super hearing and eagle vision to have seen their boss's gestures and heard that whistle from within the large lot. Either that or they were used to this kind of thing.

Diana stood aside as the four burly men muscled her old SUV through the wide gates of the car lot. They couldn't get it started, so they just put it in gear and pushed it across the road, their boss following behind as the other men steered it to an empty spot between two Italian sports cars. Boy, did it look out of place.

No sooner had they put it in park than one of the guys popped the hood and seemed to get the vehicle ready for work while the other three went back to whatever they'd been doing. The youngest guy—the one who'd taken her keys—stayed a few moments longer, rolling over a tool tray and some other gear, then he, too, melted away, back to his own work. That left her with the original man, who had to be the leader of this efficient crew.

She turned to him and offered her hand. "I'm Diana Pettigrew," she said, being bold, as was her usual habit.

The boss mechanic looked at her and took her smaller hand in one big paw. "Name's Stone."

Was that a first name or a last name? She couldn't be sure. Either way, it suited him. His sharp features looked to be carved from granite, and he was crisp and tidy in a way she hadn't expected of a working mechanic in the middle of his workday.

"You own this place?" She followed him as he walked up to the open hood of her SUV.

He spared her a glance as he started removing parts from her engine. "Nah. I just run the mechanics. Owner's name is Lance. He just got married, so he doesn't come in as much as he used to." A wide smile spread across Stone's face that could be taken a number of ways.

Diana chose to interpret it as happiness

for his boss, who sounded like a friend, as well. And maybe a bit of envy for the…uh…honeymoon activities the owner was no doubt enjoying. She didn't know how to respond to that, so she let the topic drop while Stone began an in-depth examination of the inner workings of her vehicle.

Stone didn't know what to make of the ball of dynamite standing next to him. The woman had grabbed his attention from the moment she'd entered the lot. Even before. He'd watched her walk across the street with purely masculine appreciation, but when she'd stepped over the new ward at the gate of the yard, his entire being had rung with her power.

Wow. Pretty lady packed a punch.

Thing was, he suspected she didn't know her own power. She had that same slightly lost look that Lance had sported most of the time Stone had known him. It was only when Lance had met his new mate that he'd realized his power and finally understood what he was—a phoenix shifter.

A being so rare, they were thought to be merely myth. A being of such immense power and goodness that other shifters

13

gathered to them, though they didn't know why. Stone was Alpha of a decent-sized werewolf Pack. He'd come to work for Lance years ago and had ended up getting jobs here for most of his Pack mates. The majority of the mechanics on his crew were werewolves. Likewise, the painting operation was manned by bear shifters. The front desk had a cute receptionist named Lexi who was their only lynx shifter to date, though there were a few other big cats doing various jobs around the lot, as well as a fox and some other kinds of shifter here and there. The biggest group, though, were wolves. Like Stone.

And his wolf senses were telling him things about the pretty lady whose car had conveniently broken down right in front of their gates. Had it been a coincidence? Had it been planned for some devious reason? Or had it been the hand of the Mother of All, putting Diana where she needed to be?

All that remained to be seen.

CHAPTER TWO

"I need to make a call, but my phone battery is dead," Diana said to Stone as he worked under the hood of her old car. He straightened and ushered her toward the office.

"Let's get you out of the sun," he said, hoping to put her at ease. She smelled anxious to his wolf senses, and he didn't like it. "You can use the phone inside. We also have a charging station if you want to plug in your cell for a quick recharge. And there's coffee or iced tea."

"All the comforts of home," she joked as he opened the door for her.

She still smelled nervous, and his inner wolf didn't like that at all. He was on a mission to help her calm down as he led her into the small lounge area.

"Do you want a bagel? Or some cookies?"

He liked the idea of feeding her. Maybe a bit too much. It meant something to a shifter male to want to provide food for a female. Something significant. But he didn't have time to think about that, right now. His mission was still in play. He had to help her.

"No, thanks." She made a beeline for the charging station and fumbled around with the adaptors until she found the one that fit her phone. She plugged it in with a sigh of relief, but nothing happened. No welcoming beep. No stark blue light from the screen. The thing was dead.

A look of dismay on her face brought him to her side. When those big baby blues rose to meet his gaze, his heart nearly stopped right there, on the spot. In that moment, he would do anything to make her happy. Anything to solve all her problems, no matter how big or small.

"I think it might be time for a new phone," he told her, struggling to keep his voice from going all wolfy on her. It wouldn't do to scare little red riding hood away when she'd only just got here.

"Yeah." She sighed and looked away. "It was time to get a new phone a few months ago, but I didn't have the time to go to the store. And now, I'm stuck."

"You know, you can do these things online nowadays, and they'll deliver the darn things right to your door." He tried to sound comforting rather than chastising.

"That's fine if you know what you're buying, but I'm not a technical person. I usually go and talk to the salesman and get advice before I pick a new phone." She sounded so lost, he wanted to put his arm around her shoulders and hug her close, but he didn't dare. He didn't want to send her running from him. No, this was all about making her comfortable, not pouncing on the pretty lady. Not yet, at least.

"Wait right here a moment," he told her and headed for a door leading to the back office.

He had a few wheels to put in motion

and a damsel in distress to save. Hot damn. His day had taken a left turn somewhere, but he'd be damned if he'd regret any of it. There was something really different about this lady, and it brought out instincts he hadn't thought would ever be awakened. It was a special day, indeed.

Stone left her in the middle of the posh waiting room, and Diana had to admit to herself, she was more than a little flustered by the man's presence. He was just so...male. So commanding and sure of himself. This man wouldn't object to a woman having a mind of her own, surely. Not as secure in his own skin as he seemed to be.

Then again, a man like that wouldn't look twice at a woman like Diana. He probably had sex kitten-ish girlfriends just sitting by their phones, waiting for him to call. No, a sexy guy like Stone wouldn't have to look far to find female company. And probably female company that was a lot more willing than she was to put him before all else in her life.

That was something Diana just couldn't do. Oma had to come first. In any situation

Diana found herself in, she always had to consider how it would affect her grandmother. Diana wasn't free to just go and do things whenever. Her life had to be carefully planned around her grandmother's needs, but she wouldn't have it any other way.

Sure, she might fantasize sometimes about just going to the airport and flying out to some exotic location to get away from it all for a few days, but she'd never do it. She loved her grandmother, and Diana would never abandon the responsibility that she counted as a privilege—to be able to care for her grandmother's needs as she moved down the road toward the end of her journey of this lifetime.

Oma had raised Diana after her parents' untimely death. She barely remembered them now, but Oma had stepped in and become the only person in Diana's young life that she could depend on. Oma had been there for her. Now, it was Diana's turn—and her honor—to be there for Oma.

Even if it did put a huge damper on Diana's social life...or total lack thereof.

While she'd been woolgathering, Stone must have come back into the room, because suddenly, a phone was placed into her hand. It wasn't a cell phone, but rather, a cordless model that he must've taken from the adjacent room. Diana blinked up at him. The man was silent as a cat! How had he come all the way back into the room without her even hearing the door open?

"Make your calls. I'll get the guys working on your car," he told her gently, holding her gaze with an almost tender look in his dark eyes.

Was she imagining that look? Had she been so starved for male attention that she was daydreaming gooey-eyed looks from the sexy mechanic? Man. She *had* to get out more.

"Thanks," she told him, deliberately breaking eye contact and looking down at the numbers on the phone. She dialed her grandmother's number automatically then held the handset up to her ear.

Stone was a low-down dirty eavesdropper, but he didn't let that bother him as he listened in on Diana's phone call. He was surprised when the elderly female voice answered, and then, he found himself touched by their conversation. His superior wolf hearing allowed him to hear both sides of the conversation, and he used every tool in his toolbox to learn all he could about the fascinating woman who had just walked into his life.

Diana had a grandmother she addressed as Oma. German? No, the old lady's accent was a bit softer. Holland Dutch? Possibly. It was clear from the conversation that Diana lived with the old dear and that she was going to be late getting home. The small indications of anxiety in Diana's voice made Stone want to get her back safe with her Pack—albeit a small pack of only two human females—as soon as possible.

That was at odds with his desire to keep her here, in his territory. His inner wolf decided quickly. He wanted to make her happy, and right now, being with her grandmother was what would do that best. Decision made, Stone left the lounge on silent feet and set his Pack to work.

One of the others would get the SUV rolling again, while he spent as much time as he could with Diana. He also sent one of the younger guys on an errand that wouldn't take long, and might go a long way toward fixing another of Diana's problems.

Meanwhile, Stone would sit with her, in the lounge, and try to get to know her a little better.

Why he felt compelled to do so, he didn't question. He just did. Sometimes, it was just that simple. He was a creature of instinct, and following them often led him to the right path. Hell, following his instincts had led him to take the job with Lance—the owner of this elite car repair operation. Lance had turned out to be way more magical than even Stone had expected, and he was the Alpha that all the different kinds of shifters who worked here looked to for leadership and protection.

Stone, meanwhile, was the Alpha wolf. The largest contingent of shifters on the lot were wolves, by far, so that made him sort of second in command to Lance. His position as lead mechanic made it official. Lance was new to his beast form—and it was a doozy.

Mythical phoenix shifters seldom survived their first shift. They were often pulled too strongly toward the sun and didn't come back from their first flight, being consumed in their own flame to die and start the cycle again, in a new incarnation. Phoenix shifters were so rare that Stone hadn't believed they existed until Lance had taken off, his fiery feathers shooting sparks as he'd chased the setting sun.

Only Lance's bond to his mate and his friends—the Pack he'd gathered around him in his business—had drawn him back to earth. Only those bonds of love had made him forsake the sun and return to his human existence, though he had been forever changed. Lance could shift at will now, and Stone had been helping him learn about being a shifter. He'd also been helping Lance explore the unique abilities and attributes of his beast half.

They'd already established that Lance could actually *see* evil. Not only that, but he could use his magical phoenix fire to defend his Pack and burn evil from the earth. He'd already taken out a powerful blood path mage and all her minions, leaving no trace of them behind. Stone and the others had taken care of any mundane things like the cars they'd abandoned when they chose to attack the new phoenix and all his friends. Stone was confident nobody would be able to trace their deaths to the car lot or to anyone who worked there.

He cleared his thoughts of the recent past

as he sent his people off to their tasks, then turned back to the building with a new spring in his step. He was looking forward to talking more with Diana. The wolf inside him was sitting up, alert, watching every move. It was as eager as his human side to know more about the pretty female who had entered their territory.

He deliberately made some noise with the door so she'd know he was back. She was still on the phone, just finishing up with her grandmother, from the sound of it. It was clear from the way they spoke to each other that there was genuine affection between the two.

The obvious devotion touched him deeply. Diana was a woman capable of deep caring. She'd make a good mother and a good mate for someone lucky enough to capture her heart.

Damn it all if he wasn't getting downright mushy. Stone shook himself and stepped into the lounge area. Diana said goodbye to her grandmother and held the phone out toward him.

"Thank you," she said quietly, her soft voice stroking his senses.

He walked closer, taking the phone slowly

from her hands. Their gazes met and held. He saw it then—the little spark in her eyes that said she was feeling this, too. Blessed be the Mother of All.

"Antonio's doing a quick assessment of your vehicle. He's my lead mechanic."

"I really don't think I can afford—"

Stone held up one hand to forestall her words. "This one's on me, regardless of what's wrong, okay?"

Her head tilted to the side, considering him. "Why would you do that?"

Stone shrugged, trying to keep it light, though it felt anything but. "Call it my good deed for the day."

She bit her lip, and he wanted to growl. Damn, that was sexy.

"But what if it's something big?" She looked worried, but he wasn't.

"Whatever it is, we'll get you back on the road again. I promise."

"I still don't understand why you're being so helpful." Her words were suspicious, her smile a little crooked, as if she was waiting to see if he'd pull some sort of nasty surprise on her.

Stone held both his hands up, palms outward in surrender, and decided on the honest approach—at least as far as he could without scaring her off. "Don't ask. I can't rightly explain it myself. I just want to help you, and frankly, work is light today. Fixing your car won't put us behind or anything. Gets boring just sitting around here, waiting for work to roll in. We like to keep busy."

"You may like to keep busy, but I doubt your men feel the same way," she quipped, rolling her eyes toward the lot.

"They do what I tell them," he replied, a bit of Alpha pride in his tone. "But I've known these guys a long time. We're all family, of a sort. They get just as bored as I do with inactivity."

CHAPTER THREE

Diana still couldn't figure out why Stone was being so nice to her. What was in it for him? She didn't think she was giving off vibes that would make him think he'd get paid for his kindness in any way. She'd been up front in telling him—more than once—that she probably couldn't afford such a fancy garage. Was he expecting some kind of sexual favor? Was he putting the moves on her in a strange and subtle way by fixing her car? If so, she was definitely missing something. He wasn't coming across like a creep. He actually seemed genuine, which confused her.

Nobody did something for nothing, anymore. At least, not complete strangers. She may have gotten the occasional helping hand from neighbors and friends who knew her situation, but strangers had never appeared out of the blue, ready, willing and able to help her out of a crisis. Not like this. It was almost too good to be true.

But then, she looked out the big window and saw a team of muscular guys swarming around her beat up old SUV, and she had to marvel. They certainly looked like they were repairing her car. And in record time. Her usual mechanic always made her wait a day or two—to order in parts or other nonsense. Not these people. A cart with boxes she sort of recognized as being filters and oil bottles was already sitting next to her open hood, and parts were coming out and going in at record speed.

"I see what you mean," she said, turning back to meet Stone's gaze. "I've never seen my old mechanic work that fast. Your guys appear to be on the ball. But then, I guess your usual customer has the ability to pay extra for efficient service."

Stone tilted his head, as if considering her words. It was a gesture she was coming to expect from the handsome man with the hard name...and harder body.

"While it's true we've built up a specialty business here, with an eclectic clientele, we're not snobs or rip off artists. We charge a fair wage for our work, and it doesn't matter if you drive in with a Lamborghini or lemon. That's the way the boss wants it, and frankly, that's the way we all want it."

"Your boss must be quite a man to inspire such loyalty," she observed, feeling as if she was learning quite a bit about this mechanic through his words.

Had a man ever been so candid with her on first meeting? She thought not. Stone seemed to be an above-board sort of guy, laying out his thoughts and opinions without calculating every single word out of his mouth. She liked that. She'd had too many bad run-ins with glib talkers who used words like weapons. Stone was a refreshing change.

"Lance is one of a kind, that's for sure," he told her, somehow amused by his own statement.

Before the conversation could go any

further, the door from the yard opened, and one of the mechanics she'd seen working on her car came in. He was wiping his hands on a rag and shaking his head.

"We need to order some parts," he said to Stone, shooting an apologetic glance Diana's way. "Don't think we can get them before tomorrow morning."

Stone frowned at his man, but Diana just shook her head. "My mechanic always says that and ends up keeping the car at least overnight. Luckily, he's only a few blocks from where I live, so I can usually walk home and back again, once the car's ready."

"I suspect you're more than a few blocks from home here, aren't you?" Stone asked her, turning his full attention back to her.

His expression was unexpectedly kind, and it disconcerted her a bit. Why was he so gentle with her? What had she ever done to deserve this man's compassion? What lucky star was shining down on her today? Maybe she should go buy a lottery ticket, because this kind of luck didn't last for long in her experience.

"Yeah, you could say that. I live on the other side of town. I seldom come this way, except to run the occasional errand, as I was doing today." Her skin started to itch, like something was trying to get out. Damn.

This had been happening more and more often in the past few days. She didn't know what was going on with her, but when she felt like this, she needed space and a cold shower to calm the heat that felt like it was burning her from the inside out. She didn't understand it at all, but cold water helped. A little.

Unfortunately, she was currently trapped in this repair lot at the edge of town. Not a shower or even a public fountain she could commandeer in sight. The increasing sensations made it tricky to control her own body. She wanted to scratch up against something rough. A wall. A rock face. Stone's hard body.

Oh, hell yeah! Now that sounded like the best idea she'd had yet, but she knew damn well the thought was ridiculous. She'd only just met the man. He could be married with a passel of kiddies for all she knew, and she wasn't the kind of woman to play around with a married man.

"Don't worry," Stone reassured her, and for a moment, she wondered if he knew what was going on with her skin and the tingling she couldn't control. "We'll get you a loaner car. No problem."

*

The loaner car was nothing like anything Diana had ever driven before. And Stone had insisted on escorting her across the yard, past her crappy old SUV and all those high-priced sports and luxury cars over to an area where a few other vehicles were parked. He made a big show of finding the right keys to the car he wanted to let her use then walked her over to a high-end British-made SUV that looked more like a tank than her old clunker.

This thing was built to last. It could probably go on safari and give the lions in Africa a run for their money. She had to jump up a bit to get in the driver's seat, and Stone leaned in through the open door, getting a little too close for her peace of mind, to show her the various controls. To be honest, she didn't really hear much of what he said. The man smelled so damned good, he distracted every last bit of her attention.

"And this is where the window controls

are, but you'll probably want the air conditioning. I've got it set to recirculate the cabin air. See the indicator?" He pointed to something on the center console, leaning too close. She wanted to lick him, he looked so tasty. "You with me, Red?"

"Huh...uh...what?" She didn't dare shake her head. She might hit him with her nose, he was so close to her. He turned, and their eyes met. And held. She could almost hear her own heart beating. Or was that his?

And then, he smiled. A knowing smile. A sexy smile. A slightly triumphant smile that was somehow still charming, even as it made her realize she was making this much too easy on him. If she wanted to give him the impression she was easy, she was doing a damned fine job of it—when the truth was far from it.

She'd dated her last guy for three months before they'd become intimate, and that had been more than a year ago. The relationship hadn't lasted long after they'd had sex. There had just been no spark. She'd hoped...in vain, as it turned out, and they'd both moved on.

Diana had almost given up on finding the kind of man who could stir her blood and her passions. Had she stumbled upon him here? In luxury car land of all places? Could the hunky mechanic be the man she'd been yearning for?

And what had he just called her?

"Red?" She rolled her eyes at him. "Come on, Stone. Can't you find anything more original?"

He reached over and let a lock of her wavy hair curl around his finger. The smile stayed on his handsome face as his attention was diverted for a moment to her unruly hair that seemed to want to wrap around his calloused hand the way the rest of her wanted to wrap herself around his hard body.

"It's like fire," he told her, caressing her hair gently. The care he showed was unexpected for such a hard man. It was intriguing—and a huge turn-on—that Stone could be gentle with her. It made her wonder even more what he'd be like as a lover.

"It's just hair. Red hair, I'll grant you, and naturally that way, but it's nothing special."

His gaze shot back up to meet hers, even as his voice dropped to a low, intimate tone. "I beg to differ."

Was she breathing? She thought she was

breathing, but she felt so lightheaded…

A loud, piercing whistle shattered the moment. She looked out the window of the loaner car and saw heads popping up all around the lot. She hadn't seen anyone but the guys working on her car as they crossed the yard, but there were way more people working out there than she'd thought.

Stone sighed. "Sorry, Red. That's the boss. Are you going to be all right with this vehicle?"

Secretly glad for the moment of reprieve, she nodded as he moved away. "I'll be fine. I'm used to the size, if not the luxury of this model. I'll be okay to get home and make my way back here when my car is ready."

"No need. I'll drop it off for you tomorrow, if that's all right. I couldn't help but overhear a bit of your phone call." He had the grace to look sheepish—or as sheepish as a man like him could manage. "You live with your granny, right? I suspect it's not easy to leave her on her own for long periods, so I'll bring your car back to you then drive this one back here, okay?"

She couldn't quite believe what he was saying. What had she ever done to deserve this kind of special treatment? Was some kind-hearted deity looking out for her today? She had no idea.

"That's incredibly kind of you, but you don't have to—"

He held up both hands, palms outward to halt her objections. "It'll be my pleasure. I'll call you later to give you an update, okay? And if you have any problem with this vehicle at all, you call my cell." He handed her a business card he produced from his pocket. "I wrote the number on the back. Don't hesitate to use it."

The whistle sounded again, and a few stragglers started heading for the office area where everyone else was gathering. It was an interesting way to get his employees together for a talk, but Diana just let it pass for the moment.

"Drive safe, Diana." Stone shocked her by trailing the back of his fingers over her cheek, holding her gaze as if he wanted to say more... But then, he seemed to think better of it and turned to walk away.

Diana was left holding the card.

Eventually, she put it away in her purse and started the SUV. After a moment of checking out where all the various controls were, she started making her way cautiously out of the lot and back onto the road.

It had been a strange, wonderful encounter, and she almost wouldn't believe all that had just happened...except for the vehicle she was driving. The leather steering wheel under her hands and the cold, cold air coming at her through the vents was a far cry from the plastic wheel and tepid air of her own car.

She ran the rest of her errands, then made her way home, basking in the unaccustomed luxury of the foreign car.

CHAPTER FOUR

Stone watched Diana drive away from inside the office. He knew he'd almost pushed her too far, but he hadn't wanted to let her go. His inner wolf was whining at him to go after her even now.

"What's going on?" Lance asked, coming up beside him and watching the tail lights of the Land Rover disappear onto the street beyond the lot.

"I'm not sure, but I may need some time off," Stone said, turning toward his friend who was also the owner of the car lot.

"Sounds serious," Lance observed. "Does it have anything to do with the rush job that I hear just about died at our gates an hour ago?" One eyebrow rose in question as Lance looked from Diana's SUV—which very obviously didn't belong in the yard full of high-end vehicles—then back to Stone. "It's not like you to get all worked up over a domestic clunker."

"It's not the car, but the driver," Stone admitted.

"I heard she's pretty," Lance smiled, softening his teasing words. As the Alpha wolf, Stone wasn't used to anyone teasing him, but if anyone had the power and dominance to take such liberties, it was Lance.

"She's..." Words failed Stone. He tried again. "She could be..." It was too soon to speak the very serious thoughts racing through his mind, but he had to say something. "She could be...very special. There's something about her."

"That's what I always thought about Tina," Lance commented quietly. "We've known each other since we were both in high school, you know. We didn't really interact, but I was always aware of her. She was special, even back then."

Stone had watched the relationship develop between Lance and Tina. Their mating had been cause for great celebration among the many shifters who called Lance's car lot home. Stone thought it was funny that Lance hadn't even known that shifters existed until his inner phoenix decided to make itself known.

Lance had been damned lucky to find Tina again, just when he needed her to ground him. Although she was a witch, she was a good person, and Stone had come to accept her, though usually shifters and magic users didn't mix much. She'd been there for Lance, and her love had brought him back to them all after his first shift. Her presence kept him coming back after every magical flight, and he was getting better and better at becoming the power he had always been meant to be.

Lance was the focus of their larger Pack. Stone might be Alpha of the wolf Pack, but Lance was the Alpha over all of them. Stone hadn't understood it before Lance's inner phoenix had been revealed, but now, it all make perfect sense. Stone and his wolves—

along with the other shifters of various species—had been drawn to the phoenix to both protect it and to gain protection from it. They were all stronger together than they were apart, and they'd formed a weird sort of multi-species family with a witch as den mother.

"I'm not sure Diana is to me what Tina is to you," Stone told his friend as he turned away from the window. "But she could be."

Lance clapped Stone on the back as they made their way into the gathering of their people. He cared about these people—even the bears, who were sometimes a bit irritating to his wolf senses—but his inner wolf was starting to scratch at his insides, wanting to follow Diana.

Soon, he promised his impatient furry side. *Tonight, we'll take a little run over by Diana's place. And maybe we'll learn a bit more about her and her granny.*

*

Diana parked the luxury SUV and patted the door frame before leaving it behind. It was such a nice vehicle. Too bad she couldn't afford something like it. Heck, she couldn't even afford a new domestic car, much less something imported. But it was sure a nice treat for a change. She just couldn't let herself get used to it.

Diana made sure to secure the garage before walking into the condo she shared with her grandmother. Oma would probably want to know all about her adventure, but first, Diana had to get a start on dinner. Oma couldn't really handle cooking every day, so they split the duties. Diana would do anything that required chopping or lifting, and stove stuff was all Diana's. But Oma could handle making sandwiches for lunch or things of that nature.

Tonight, they were having turkey Diana had prepared the other day, but she was making fresh side dishes to go with it. She'd become expert at portioning out things so that the two of them could use all the food before it went bad. It was difficult when most items in the market were intended for families with lots of mouths to feed. Diana had to make judgments on what would work best for just the two of them, and if she judged wrong, she ended up wasting a lot of money they didn't have on food that went bad before they could use it all.

Moving in with Oma had required a steep learning curve. Diana had had to figure out how to run a household that consisted of just two women, when one of them couldn't really do much for herself anymore, and needed a lot of assistance. It had been a drastic change for Diana, who had been used to going wherever the wind took her, whenever the mood struck. Now, she had to plan every trip and every move she made around her grandmother's wellbeing.

It was difficult, at times, but she didn't begrudge Oma this time. It was an honor to help her grandmother, and frankly, sharing expenses made it possible to live in this nice, quiet community, which soothed Diana's nerves. The low-rent neighborhood she'd lived in before was a lot noisier and less safe. Money was still tight, but by moving in together, they'd been able to pool their resources, so it was a win-win for both of them location wise.

Diana kissed her grandmother hello on her way to the kitchen. Oma was parked in her recliner in front of the television, as usual, but the elderly lady got up and followed Diana into the kitchen, which was unusual. Then again, today had been an unusual day all around. Diana bustled around the kitchen, getting things going while Oma took a seat at the breakfast bar and watched.

"So, what about this man you met today?" she finally said, a knowing gleam in her blue-grey eyes.

"Why don't you tell me?" Diana challenged with a grin. "You've got that look on your face that tells me you saw something."

Oma's clairvoyance was sporadic, but strong enough that Diana was used to the signs that her grandmother had seen something. Diana had grown up knowing about magic. Oma came from a long line of witches, though the power often skipped a generation or wasn't as potent in one generation or another. Diana herself didn't have any magic to speak of, but she could sense it, sometimes.

Oma's mother had been a true power. Diana had grown up hearing stories about her great-grandmother and the amazing things she could do, as well as the amazing people she had known. To Diana, shifters were the stuff of her bedtime stories, but unlike most girls, Diana had grown up knowing that such beings existed and weren't just fairy stories.

Not that she'd ever knowingly met any. She'd suspected a time or two, but it would be the height of rudeness to just flat out ask an acquaintance if they could howl at the moon in animal form, whenever they felt like it. No, that wouldn't do at all. So, Diana had kept her suspicions to herself and had just gone about her business.

Come to think of it...there had been something kind of wild in the men she'd seen at the car lot today. She wondered idly if maybe they were shifters of some kind, but she'd likely never know for sure. Oh, well. Maybe Oma has seen something that could help solve that mystery.

"He's a magic man," Oma said, her tone utterly serious, though there was a sparkle in her eye. "With a complex spirit and allegiances to powers even greater than his own. He understands things about the unseen world that we do not. Things that you, particularly, may need to know one day soon."

Diana was used to her grandmother speaking in riddles when describing her visions, but that didn't make it any easier. As always, Diana felt a bit annoyed with her lack of understanding. What did her grandmother's words really *mean*? It sure sounded as if they were important, this time. More important than usual—especially for Diana. Was it a warning or simply a foretelling that her new acquaintance with Stone would last longer than just a day or two?

"The whole place felt special. I think there were wards on the entrance," Diana admitted as she sat down for a moment near her grandmother.

"There probably were. I saw a man standing beside a being of fire and benevolence. And you were somehow connected to that fire being, but it was the man beside him that I saw most clearly. He's interested in you. And he's part of the puzzle of you, somehow."

Oma had often spoken about how Diana was a puzzle. She was used to it by now, though the idea that there was something wrong, or different, about her had often troubled her as a child.

They talked more about the nebulous vision over dinner as night fell outside. After eating, Oma went back into the living room while Diana set the kitchen to rights. She puttered around, cleaning things that were already clean, thinking about everything that had happened that day. She couldn't keep her mind from focusing on Stone. He was such an enigma, and a sexy one at that.

As she was about to leave the kitchen and join Oma in the living room, her senses sprang to life. Something was outside. Watching her.

She shut off the lights and sidled up to the window, looking out from the side to see if she could catch any movement out in the backyard. Eventually, her patience was rewarded.

There was a wolf at the back door.

CHAPTER FIVE

Diana crept into the living room and kept her voice low.

"Oma, there's a wolf outside."

Her grandmother didn't seem surprised. "That explains a lot." She set her needlepoint down on the side table and shook her head. "You'd better go let him in and give him something to wear. Mama always said their clothes don't shift with them," Oma advised.

"You mean he's a shifter?" Diana just

barely breathed the words.

"You know who it is, don't you?" Her grandmother sent her a knowing look. "It's the man from earlier. He's come to call. Don't keep him waiting. I want to meet him."

Diana shook her head and grabbed a bath towel on the way past the bathroom then went into the kitchen. "I hope you're right about this. Otherwise, I could get mauled."

"You won't get mauled," her grandmother said in an exasperated tone laced with laughter. "You'll see."

"It's a good thing I trust you with my life," Diana muttered and threw open the back door.

When Diana opened the back door and caught Stone lurking on her back porch, he didn't scent fear from her, only interest. His furry ears perked up and heard her sigh.

"If that really is you, Stone, then you'd better change and come on in. Oma wants to meet you." She draped a large white towel over the rail to the back porch then retreated to the door, closing it behind her but failing to lock it.

Well, didn't that beat all? She knew about

shifters. What in the world did that mean?

Stone supposed there was only one way to find out. He shifted and grabbed the towel, wrapping it around his hips as he walked up to the unlocked door and opened it. There was no tingle of magic as he crossed the threshold, but that didn't mean much. Maybe the magic in this house was more subtle than to have noisy wards on every entrance. He was definitely intrigued to find out what the story was with little red and her granny.

And here he was, their personal big bad wolf, come to call. Stone would have chuckled if he wasn't so preoccupied with the scents in the house. Turkey dinner. He could still smell traces of it in the kitchen as he walked in.

He shut the back door behind himself then followed his senses to the living room where Diana was standing next to her granny's recliner. He could see the resemblance, though the granny's hair was white with a golden sheen. They shared the fine bone structure that marked them as relatives.

"Welcome, young man. I am Hetty van Dunk, and you've already met my granddaughter, Diana Pettigrew. You are a werewolf."

"And you are…witches?" Stone asked, standing in the entry to the living room, wanting to get all his facts straight before he got in any deeper.

"Oh, not really. I mean, we both carry the genes but are a bit short on the talent." Hetty's words rang with truth, and Stone's senses didn't detect the various telltales of lies. "My mother was a very potent witch in her time, but I didn't inherit her power. I only have a minor gift of clairvoyance, and it's been showing me you—alongside a being of intense power who burns with the fire of Light."

Well, if that wasn't a description of Lance, Stone didn't know what was. The old woman might actually have the gift of Sight as she believed.

"Your mother knew about my kind?" he asked, skirting the discussion of Lance for the moment.

He honestly hadn't expected this sort of reception. In fact, he hadn't intended to interact with Diana and her granny at all, but having been caught in the act, so to speak, he had little choice but to play out this scenario.

"Oh, yes. My mother served as priestess to a large flight of owls in Northern Europe in her day. She was friendly mainly with flight shifters, but she told me all about the other kinds of shapeshifters when I was growing up. She had hope I would follow in her footsteps, but as I reached maturity and didn't develop any talent other than the clairvoyance, we both knew that path was not meant for me."

"And you taught your granddaughter what your mother had taught you, even though she didn't have the gift?" Stone inquired.

"My mother taught me first," Diana put in, her hand on her grandmother's shoulder in a show of support, or perhaps to offer comfort to the older lady.

"My daughter, Sophie, was more gifted than me, and my mother was still around while Sophie was young. Sophie learned a lot from her. Frankly, her power was more than I could handle, but it proved to me why my mother thought it was so important to pass on the knowledge in our line, even to those of us not as magically gifted. You see, we never know when a gift like my mother's or my daughter's will come along. Imagine how it would be for a witch to be born into a generation with no knowledge of what she was or the power she could wield."

Stone thought about that for a moment while the old lady paused and realized the results wouldn't be good. Such power could easily consume a person or cause harm to those around them. It had to be trained and controlled when it developed. Passing on the family heritage and the knowledge of Others was a good idea in this family, since the magic seemed to touch them so sporadically.

"As it is, with what little power we can command, we serve the Light. Where do you stand, my werewolf friend?" Hetty challenged him, a hard glint in her blue eyes.

"I, and my Pack, stand in the Lady's Light," he declared, proud in his heart that he and every single one of his men had been tested and proven their worth. They had fought and prevailed against evil when it had come for them, and they protected and followed the phoenix, whose flame burned with the pure Light of the Goddess Herself.

Hetty smiled. "I like the conviction in your voice when you say that, young man. Now, tell me. What is your name?"

"Stone, ma'am," he supplied immediately,

liking the old lady more with each passing moment.

"Stone? Is that a first name or a surname?" Hetty looked a bit scandalized by his lack of detail.

"Forgive me, ma'am. I'm Adam Stone, Alpha of the Desert Valley Pack."

Both women wore identical raised-eyebrow expressions. Oh yeah, the family resemblance was strong with these two. His inner wolf was as amused by their response as his human half.

Hetty looked up at her granddaughter. "Your friend here is not just a werewolf, but the leader of the Pack." After a moment of silent communication between the two, Hetty turned back to him. "Now, tell me, young man. Why did you seek my granddaughter out tonight?"

"She's a puzzle, ma'am, and I wanted more information. I didn't intend to be spotted, much less invited inside, or I would've arranged for some clothes." He tilted his head and nodded downward toward the towel that was his only covering.

Normally, he didn't give a damn about being naked. Most shifters accepted skin and fur in equal measure. But one didn't just traipse into an elderly grandmother's house—a human one, at that—swinging in the breeze. Arranging for proper clothing when meeting elders was a sign of respect and care that spoke a lot about a person. Stone's mother had impressed upon him the need for good manners and respect for one's elders.

"What puzzled you about my granddaughter, Alpha?" Hetty delved for answers that made Stone itch a bit, because he wasn't sure exactly how to describe it—especially to the woman's granny.

He looked around at the quaint furnishings in the condo to buy time, showing a bit of his discomfort. The furniture was functional and well cared for, but not exactly expensive. Judging by the car and now, the house, these women were just about getting by. Nothing frivolous or expensive for them. That made Stone's inner wolf want to hunt and provide dinner for them. Protective instincts rose up in him that should have worried him a bit...but somehow, they didn't. It felt right to be protective of this female and her granny. Odd, that, but there it was.

"I sensed magic around her, but I wasn't

sure what kind it was," he told the old woman, prevaricating a bit. Honestly, Diana's power—though tiny compared to Lance—felt almost the same. Burning. Pure. Intensely magical. Diana felt a bit the way Lance had before his transformation into the phoenix. "Tell me, are there any shifters in your family line, ma'am?"

Hetty's eyes narrowed. "Her magic feels like shifter magic to you?"

Stone shrugged. "A bit. It's somewhat familiar, but very muted. As if hidden. Maybe latent."

Hetty's gaze scrutinized him. A lesser man would probably be quaking before that inspection, but Stone was Alpha wolf hereabouts. He knew how to hold his own.

"Latent, you say?" Hetty looked up at her granddaughter. "I sometimes wish my own gift was stronger so I could have guided you better. It's always possible you're a late bloomer, sweetheart."

"Or it could just be latent, like Mr. Stone said," Diana put in with a sigh. "Either way, it doesn't matter. What will be, will be. I gave up looking for fairies around every mushroom circle long ago."

"Oh, dear." Hetty took Diana's hand in

hers and patted it. "I wish you wouldn't say things like that. I fear my frailty has made you far too practical. Your heart should still be filled with wonder and expectation at your age."

Diana laughed and leaned down to kiss her grandmother's cheek. There was obviously a lot of love between the two women, and Stone felt privileged to witness it. When Diana straightened, Hetty started working her way up out of the chair. Diana helped her until Hetty was standing, facing Stone.

"I'm going to leave you two to talk a bit. You didn't come all this way to see me, I'm sure." Hetty smiled at him, and her eyes twinkled.

"Ma'am," Stone said, nodding respectfully as Hetty shuffled out of the room, leaning heavily on her cane.

And then, he had what he really wanted. He was alone with the mysterious and lovely Diana.

CHAPTER SIX

Silence fell as soon as her grandmother left the room, and Diana was even more acutely aware that Stone was wearing nothing but one of her bath towels slung precariously low around his narrow hips. She had to stop herself from looking at his muscular legs and washboard abs, but what she'd seen already was drool-worthy.

For a man who could become a wolf at will, he had surprisingly little hair on his body, but the sexy line that arrowed lightly down beneath the top of the towel made her think scandalous thoughts. He had scars, too. More than a few. She wondered what kind of life he'd led that had brought about those puckered lines of various vintages. Some were clearly old and well-healed. Some were newer. One thing was certain. This man had seen a great deal of fighting in his lifetime.

She realized she was staring again, and shook herself out of it. This would never do. And the tiny smirk of amusement on his lips told her he'd caught her staring, too. Darn it.

"Can I get you something to drink? Coffee? Tea?" she offered, remembering her manners, even though she'd never had a mostly naked werewolf visitor in her home before.

"I don't suppose you have any beer in the house," Stone said, tilting his head toward the kitchen in a questioning way.

"Not right now," she replied.

He snorted, laughing at her response. "Not ever, I suspect."

She stood up straighter, slightly offended by his assumption, though she wasn't sure why. "Occasionally, Oma likes to cook Dutch food, and there are certain dishes that are complemented by a cold beer. Imported from the old country, of course." Great. Now, she sounded like a snob.

"Which old country is that? Germany?"

"Please. Oma's a *van* not a *von*. She was born in the Netherlands, but the family came here after World War Two." What in the *world* was she talking about? She had a *mostly naked werewolf* in her house, for heaven's sake! Why was she talking about such mundane matters? "Why did you really come here tonight, Mr. Stone?"

"It's just Stone. Or I guess you could call me Adam, but nobody else does. Not anymore. Not since my mama passed on." Was that vulnerability that flashed through his gaze for a moment, or was she reading things into his expression that she wanted to see? Or, worse yet, was he somehow subtly manipulating her?

No. She refused to think ill of the man just because she was afraid. Exactly what she was afraid of, she wasn't quite sure, but her emotions had been spinning out of control lately, and she'd been starting at shadows for weeks now. Fear was almost her constant companion, but she wouldn't let it get the best of her. Not if she could help it.

"I spent a lot of time in the military," he went on to explain. "Getting called by your last name is pretty standard in that environment, and the guys I hang out with all have similar backgrounds, so the pattern held, even though we're strictly civilians now."

"I didn't know that shifters served in the military," she said inanely, trying to buy some time to calm her thoughts and control her emotions.

"A lot of us find channeling our aggression to work for Uncle Sam a productive way to spend the years when we're learning control over our human sides. In general, we're natural born fighters, so it's good to learn discipline, and the military excels at that."

"But does anyone in the government or the higher ranks know about...what you are?" Now, she was just intrigued.

She hadn't expected their conversation to go in this direction but was fascinated by the implications. Did certain humans know about shifters and use their abilities in secret to defend the country? Or was shifter culture working behind the scenes, existing within the framework of the human military, without anybody being the wiser?

"There's one very high-ranking fellow who knows about us and uses our skills to their greatest potential, but I doubt anybody else knows what's really going on. Not any regular folk, at any rate. This man who knows—he's magical, too. Some sort of elemental power, from all accounts."

"Wow." Diana could've kicked herself when the word left her lips. *Way to sound intelligent, Di. Really.* She cleared her throat and tried again. "I mean, that's very interesting, but you still haven't answered my question. Why did you come here?"

He paused, regarding her with narrowed eyes for a moment before responding. "I wanted to see you again."

Hmm. She thought about that, her heart beginning a little pitter-patter of excitement at the idea that they sexy man might actually be interested in her as a woman. Or, maybe, he was just intrigued by the puzzle of her latent power. The momentary thrill dissipated. Why in the world would this god-like being be interested in plain old her? Yeah, right.

"You're going to see me tomorrow," she reminded him, trying to sound casual.

"I didn't want to wait." He took a step forward, closing the distance between them slowly.

Why was he coming closer? She was confused as that little feeling of exhilaration returned, hopeful, but afraid to hope. Maybe he was just restless, but it sure looked like he was…sort of…stalking her.

His gaze never left hers as he moved another step closer.

"You intrigue me, Diana," he said, his voice a low growl that did funny things to her insides. "Man and wolf, I want to know more about you." He took another step closer. "I thought maybe, I could sniff around a bit outside your home to learn more. I never expected to be invited in, but now that I'm here…" He was so close now, she could feel the intense heat of him, just inches away from her.

His scent was compelling. Somehow familiar, and very attractive. Hot-blooded, sexy man laced with desert sage and a faint hint of motor oil. A working man's scent that was both honest and incredibly erotic.

"Do you feel it? This magic that sparks between us when we're near like this?" he asked, sliding one big hand around her waist and pulling her unresisting body closer one inch at a time.

She felt something. Tickling her senses. Something powerful. Something that she felt, in her heart, could be intensely beautiful if she knew how to see it. Lost for words, she nodded her agreement, moving closer as he drew her, wanting to know his touch, his kiss, like she'd never wanted any man before.

It was a physical ache that she sensed only Stone could cure. She went willingly into his embrace, her hands landing on his hard-muscled chest and then exploring. His skin was a tactile delight, and he seemed to like the way she stroked up to his shoulders, twining her hands around his neck as his head descended to touch his lips to hers.

She was lost completely in his kiss, but she felt something break open inside her, as if some power was acknowledging Stone's presence and accepting the passion between them with a welcoming sigh. She felt empowered by his kiss, emboldened by his embrace. She felt womanly, and for the first time in her life, she felt like the mythical huntress she'd been named for.

Diana. Goddess of the hunt, the moon, and nature in the Roman pantheon. Said to have power over animals. She wondered if that included power over sexy werewolves who kissed like Eros himself. She was mixing up her Greeks and Romans, but she didn't care at the moment.

The world ceased to exist, except for the man who held her so securely in his arms and the kiss that seemed to last for eternity but ended much too soon. She felt so safe in Stone's embrace. She didn't want it to end, but he drew back, releasing her lips to gaze down into her eyes.

"Tell me you felt that," he whispered. "There's magic between us, woman, and I want more."

He held her for a long moment, and she wondered if he was going to take that *more* right then and there. She wouldn't have minded, except for the fact that her grandmother was in the house and could come back into the living room at any moment.

That thought sobered her a little bit, so that when Stone moved farther away, separating their bodies by slow increments, she was steadier on her feet. She probably would've fallen on her nose if he had let her go right away, and the sexy smile on his face said he probably knew that and was pleased by her reaction to his kiss.

"Have lunch with me tomorrow," he invited, that sexy smile still firmly in place. "I'll bring your car back around noon, and we can go someplace nice for a meal. What do you say?"

A lunch date? The werewolf who had just kissed her senseless wanted to do something as tame as take her to lunch? Hmm. Maybe he was giving her a little space to get used to him before he went after that *more* he had talked about. She wasn't sure whether to wring her hands in frustration—because she wanted more too, dammit—or thank him for being a gentleman and giving her time to get to know him before she gave in to impulse and jumped his bones in a most uncharacteristic—until now—display of sexual aggression.

But there was her grandmother to consider. She'd have to arrange things to make this happen. Then again, Oma was forever encouraging her to go out and do things on her own. She was well aware that Diana's social life suffered.

"Okay. Lunch." Wow. She'd just agreed to have lunch with the biggest, baddest-assed werewolf ever. *Take that, fear! You ain't the boss of me.*

Trailing one hand down her arm, he took hold of her hand as they walked slowly back toward the kitchen and the back door of the condo. Damn. He was going to leave. She wished she could drag him to her room and convince him to drop the gentlemanly impulses, but Oma would be scandalized. The walls in this condo were pretty thin, and sound carried in the dark hours of the night. Unfortunately.

When he stopped near the closed door to the small back porch, he turned to her, drawing her into his arms loosely, this time. His big hands were on her hips, and her hands went to his shoulders, leaving space between them but allowing his warmth to soothe her. He was such a confident man. She liked the way he held himself, sure of his place in the world. She needed a bit of that mojo.

Maybe…just maybe…he could help her figure some of that out. If they got to know each other better, that is. Some of his self-assurance might just rub off on her a bit. Heaven knew, she could use it. Especially now, when everything seemed to be getting so weird in her life with these strange yearnings for the heat of the desert and dreams of flying into the sun. She had no idea what it all meant.

"I'll come for you at noon," he told her softly, raising one hand to brush his fingers gently over her cheek. "Wear something sexy. Heels, if you have them. I want to take you someplace special."

"I'll look forward to it." As the words left her mouth, she knew she would think of nothing else every waking moment until she saw him again. What a rush! She felt giddy with excitement in a way she hadn't experienced since she was a kid.

He leaned in and kissed her gently, one finger under her chin. Could he feel her trembling? She wanted so much more but knew it was impossible just at the moment. He clearly understood the limitations of the situation, which was totally sweet. Just like his lingering kiss.

"I'll see you tomorrow, then," he said in that soft, growly voice that did shivery things to her insides. "Lock this door behind me."

He opened the back door quietly and padded onto the private porch. He was down the steps and in the darkness beyond the porch in another heartbeat. The man could move both swiftly and silently when he wanted to. She thought he was gone, until out of the darkness, her bath towel landed over the porch rail, and she could just hear him whisper.

"Close the door, Diana."

She started a bit, surprised he was still there, though she couldn't see him. She felt a tingle of magic brush lightly against her senses, and then, she thought she saw the faint reflection of canine eyes just beyond the porch steps. He'd shifted, she realized, and was watching until she followed his instructions.

She stepped out onto the porch, feeling a bit defiant as she reached for the towel, but he stayed hidden. She clearly wasn't going to see his wolf form up close and personal that night, though she was very intrigued by the entire concept.

Diana retrieved the towel and went back inside. "Goodnight, Adam," she whispered, just before she closed and locked the door.

It felt strange to call him by the first name he claimed nobody used. Strange and special. Like it was a secret just between them. Intimate.

The first of many intimacies, she hoped, then realized she was almost totally committed in her own mind to making love with the sexy shifter. Never before had she fallen so hard, so fast. Was it part of his magic that he could seduce her so easily? Or was it just kismet. Meant to be.

That's what it felt like. As if she'd been waiting for him all her life.

But that was ridiculous. One didn't just meet their soul mate by accident. Or, rather, by her car breaking down in exactly the right spot. Did they?

CHAPTER SEVEN

Diana breezed through her evening chores, locked up the condo and set the dishwasher to run, then went to bed. Her grandmother stayed in her room, which surprised Diana a bit, but maybe Oma just wanted to give her some space. It was odd how her senses were reeling from just a kiss, but there was something incredibly special about Adam Stone and the way he touched her. Something magical.

She'd have to ask Oma about the whole

concept of two magical beings interacting. Could being with Stone have some sort of effect on Diana's own latent magical heritage? Could his influence be bad for her, somehow? She didn't think so. In fact, just being near him felt really, really good. But was there some kind of influence his magic might exert over her?

There was definitely a spark between them. She'd never ignited so quickly in a man's arms. And she'd never come to the conclusion that she would jump a man's bones at her earliest opportunity. Of course, she'd never been with a man as compelling as the Alpha werewolf before. In comparison to Stone, all of her ex-boyfriends had been total wimps.

They hadn't been. Not really. But Stone was just too male. Every other man paled in comparison. Maybe it wasn't fair to her exes to ask mere humans to measure up to an Alpha wolf in his prime. Yeah, that was probably it. Adam was just something else altogether. More male. More attractive. More intense. An absolute seduction to everything that was female in her.

Mmmm. She couldn't wait to get him naked and alone.

That was the thought that sent her into dreamland, where she imagined romping through a field of flowers with a furry companion before lying down in a meadow with Adam over her, making love to her. She woke at dawn, her body on fire as never before. On fire with desire for Adam, but also enflamed with the yearning that had no name for the desert and...the sun.

It seemed to be worse now than it had ever been. Had kissing Adam last night somehow triggered it?

She got out of bed and stood by her window, watching the sun rise. She wanted to smash through the glass and jump into the sun, crazy as that sounded. Where were these thoughts and impulses coming from? Things were getting weirder every day, and she seldom slept past sunrise lately. It was as if the waking of the sun called to her. Compelled her.

It was getting harder to resist leaving the house and going out into the desert to just...commune...or something...with the light and heat of it. Was she going bonkers? She just wasn't sure.

But today, she had something to distract her from the compulsion. She was going to lunch with a sexy werewolf. Adam.

She still thought of him as Stone from time to time, but she liked the intimacy of calling him Adam—even in her own mind— more and more. Adam. The first man. Actually, the first man in her life to ever evoke such a spectacular response.

She remembered the dreams she'd had most of the night about being with him in his wolf form and making love to him in his human form. He had the most amazing body. That towel hadn't covered up much, and it had left plenty for her to feast her eyes on—and fuel her imagination. She'd dreamed of licking her way down his washboard abs…and more.

Just remembering her brazen dream behavior made her move away from the window and the heat of the oncoming sun. She took a cold shower—as she had many mornings of late when she woke up feeling something like the sun burning just beneath her skin—but this morning, it had the added effect of cooling her overheated libido. A bit.

She got dressed and then went down to the kitchen to make breakfast for Oma and herself. Routine. Normal. When lunch promised to be anything but normal. Yay!

Her inner hussy was already planning what she'd wear in hopes of seducing the big werewolf into naughty behavior. She hoped he had more than just a quick meal in a public restaurant in mind. She was hoping he had someplace private they could go where she could follow the driving impulse to take a walk on the wild side…with him.

Diana tried hard not to let anything of her scandalous inner thoughts show when she and Oma shared breakfast. Her grandmother teased her a bit about the werewolf before settling in to discuss what she knew of shifters. Oma seemed to want to prepare Diana for whatever might happen by telling her everything she could remember of what her mother had taught her about the various magical races.

So, the morning turned into a time of learning where Diana solidified some of the things she remembered hearing before and learned some enticing new facets of shifter lore. It was fascinating, and the time passed all too fast.

Before she knew it, it was time for her to search through her closet for something sexy, as instructed. She had a LBD somewhere. It was a rule she and her schoolmates had come up with that she'd always abided by—a girl had to have at least one Little Black Dress in her closet at all times, in case the opportunity came up to do something special.

Well, lunch with a sexy Alpha werewolf was certainly special. If that didn't call for application of the LBD, nothing did! She even had heels that went perfectly with her dress. Now, if she could just find them. She wasn't the neatest of people, and she hadn't worn the LBD in…darn it…more than a year, probably.

There! There it was! Diana took hold of the hangar and inspected the dress. It looked okay. Hopefully, it still fit the way it should. And there were the matching heels. Great! She took both into the bathroom where she took another shower and then groomed herself a bit more than she had in a while—just in case.

By eleven forty-five, she was ready. Ready and trying hard not to pace. Oma was getting ready herself. She had arranged to spend the afternoon with her friend, Mrs. Peabody. She said they were going to be trying out a new embroidery technique and she would be there all afternoon, including the customary four o'clock tea time, so Diana was not to worry about her.

With those marching orders—given with a wink—Diana was able to look forward to her afternoon guilt-free. Oma had a definite spring in her step as she bustled over to the condo next door at exactly ten minutes to twelve. Diana suspected Oma and Mrs. Peabody would be watching every move Stone and she made through the lace curtains next door, probably giving each other a running commentary on his manners, his appearance, the way they looked together and the way they looked at each other. Microscopes had nothing on her grandmother's level of scrutiny and well-developed spying techniques.

Just before twelve, Diana saw her old SUV round the corner onto her street. Not that she'd been watching out the window—through their own set of lace curtains. Rushing out of sight of the window, she smoothed her skirt a bit and checked her hair one last time in the mirror by the door. Her purse was on the little console table, all ready to go. Now, all she had to do was keep herself together until he walked up to the door and try not to make a fool of herself when she saw him.

The doorbell rang, and she mentally counted to five before opening the door. There he was. As delicious looking as the day before, but this time, the smile on his face was knowing. He knew, after all, how she kissed, how she responded to his touch. Diana fought a blush as he looked her up and down then let out a low wolf whistle.

"You're gorgeous, Red," he said, his voice rumbling with the appreciative growl of a wolf.

"Thanks. You're not so bad yourself," she replied, noting the effort he'd taken with his own appearance. Dress slacks had replaced the jeans he'd worn the day before, paired with a white dress shirt. He looked downright yummy in a business-y sort of way.

When he handed her the keys to her SUV, she was a little surprised, but then, she remembered what he'd said yesterday. "Test drive, right?"

"Exactly. It's your vehicle. You know it best. I want to be sure you're totally happy with the way it runs, which means I want you to put her through her paces." He ushered her down the front walk after she closed and locked the front door, the perfect gentleman.

Diana could see the curtains fluttering next door as he opened the driver's side door for her and waited for her to get in. He was both solicitous and polite, which she knew was scoring him big points with the older generation. Come to think of it, his classy manners were scoring him big points with her, as well.

He was a man of hidden depths. Yesterday, she would have scoffed to think of the denim-clad mechanic dressed like a yuppie businessman. Today, she was having a hard time controlling her drool reflex whenever she looked at him. He was just that hot. H. O. T.

She got behind the wheel of her old car, and he closed the door for her. He scooted around the other side and climbed into the passenger seat, and suddenly, the spacious cabin seemed a whole lot smaller. And hotter. She reached over to crank up the A/C another notch, but she wasn't all that confident it would help.

Diana started the car, surprised when the usually cranky engine turned right over and began to purr. "What the heck?" she mused as she put the car in gear. It didn't stick! In fact, the obstreperous transmission didn't balk at all as she eased into drive and began rolling down the road. "What did you *do* to this car?"

"Just gave her a little TLC. She's basically sound and sturdy. She just hasn't been treated very nicely over the past few years. Whichever garage you were using wasn't really doing all they should have been," Stone told her.

"Seriously? I sure paid them enough and waited endlessly for parts and then for the work to be done," she muttered, feeling a little anger at her old mechanic.

"Well, don't worry about that now. You have any problems in the future, you know where to go." He sounded just the tiniest bit smug—and sure of himself. Hmm.

"This was a one-off," she told him ruefully. "I can't afford to use your garage on a regular basis. It's pretty obvious you guys cater to the luxury and high-end sports car crowd."

"Sure, those cars are fun to work on— especially the supercars—but when it comes down to it, an engine is an engine, and they all need care from time to time. You don't have to go to the garage if you don't want. Consider me your personal mechanic from here on out."

She stopped at a red light and turned to look at him. "Why?" She couldn't help but ask. "Why would you do that for me?"

Stone shrugged, as if his answer didn't matter. "Let's just say for now, that I like your granny and want to be sure you have adequate transport to help her. Think of it as my good deed." One side of his mouth quirked up in a smile. "Besides, if you don't call me when you need your next oil change, you know I'll just sneak into your garage in the middle of the night and do it anyway."

His words sparked a laugh from her. She could just see him skulking around like a ninja, fixing her car.

"I can only imagine what Mrs. Peabody would think." Diana shook her head and chuckled.

CHAPTER EIGHT

"Who? The little old lady next door. Biggest damn teapot collection on her kitchen shelves I've ever seen?" Stone asked.

"How'd you see her teapot collection?" Diana glanced at him in surprise.

He pointed to his eyes. "My, granny. What big eyes you have."

She puzzled his words out for a moment and realized he was referring to himself as the wolf in the old fairy tale. She wondered idly if the fairy tale actually had something to do with shifters, but shook her head. He was implying something even more interesting.

"Do you mean to say that werewolves have keener eyesight than regular people?" Again, she glanced at him, even as she drove, following his instructions on where to turn.

"All the senses, really. We're closer to our animal nature than others." He shrugged off his words as if they weren't that important, but to Diana, they were bringing back memories of the stories her grandmother had told her.

"I've heard a little about that," she said quietly. "Oma told me things her mother had taught her about shifters, but I've never met any before."

"None that you knew about," he corrected her gently.

"I thought you guys were really rare," she countered.

"Not as rare as one might think. I bet you've crossed paths with shifters before and just didn't realize it."

"The world is a funny place," she mused aloud. "When I was little, I imagined every other person I met was a shapeshifter, but as I grew up and never had any confirmation, I just sort of put all that behind me as fanciful childhood imagination."

"Maybe not as fanciful as you thought, eh?" He sent her a wolfish grin as she glanced at him again.

She followed his instructions to turn again, though he still refused to tell her exactly where they were going. After the next quick turn, she started recognizing the area and was able to guess.

"Alfredo's? We're going to Alfredo's?" She'd always wanted to try the upscale eatery, but her budget didn't really stretch that far.

"The very same," he agreed affably. "Ever been there before?"

"In my dreams," she told him. "They'll probably want me to drive around to the service entrance rather than pull up to the valet stand in this jalopy."

"Hey, don't call her names. Your car and I made friends last night as I was fixing her up for you. She's got a good heart under the years of neglect by your former mechanic."

She had to chuckle at his weird sense of humor—and the fact that he was so sure of himself that he didn't even question that she would never go back to her old mechanic. She wouldn't. But that was more to do with the revelation that he hadn't been doing right by her SUV. She wasn't going to pay for shoddy service anymore. Whether or not she'd take the car to Stone remained to be seen.

"You worked on my car last night?" she asked, rather than delve into her other lines of thought. She didn't want to argue with him about where her car would be fixed just yet because that question was still an open one in her own mind.

"Yeah, after I left you, I went back to the shop and put in a few hours." He said it like it was no big deal, but she was a little appalled that he'd lost sleep over her old car.

"You didn't have to do that," she told him.

"Yeah, actually, I did. Old Bessie here needed a lot of TLC." He paused for a moment as the restaurant came in sight. "And I couldn't sleep anyway. Too much to think about. Working on the car helped settle my mind. Work is my way of de-stressing."

She didn't have time to ask him more about that as they came to the entrance of the upscale restaurant. He directed her to pull into the valet lane, and the sandy-haired youngster who manned the valet stand didn't even blink an eye when she drove in. His young face split into a wide grin when he saw Stone, though.

"Alph—uh—Mr. Stone," the boy greeted him, looking sharply at Diana before altering his words.

Hot damn. The kid had to be a shifter. Or, at least, he knew about shifters enough to know that Stone was an Alpha. Wow.

"Hey Peter, how's school going?" Stone reached out and shook the teenager's hand, giving him a reassuring smile. Diana watched as the kid relaxed.

"I settled on Berkley for college since it's not too far and has a great program. Mom and Dad are just happy I didn't decide on one of the East Coast schools that accepted me," he admitted with a grin. "But I wouldn't want to be that far from home anyway."

"That's great, Pete." Stone touched the boy's shoulder, almost like a pat on the back. "Is Maximo in the kitchen today?"

"Where else would he be? It's his favorite place in the whole universe." Peter rolled his eyes, but his smile was contagious.

"Peter, this is Diana, and this is her car

that I was up all night fixing." The message was pretty clear as Diana handed over her keys to the teen.

"I'll take extra special care, Alph—uh—Mr. Stone."

Diana shook her head as the kid made a quick getaway after that last fumble, just about vaulting into the driver's seat and speeding away.

"Is he one of yours?" Diana asked Stone quietly.

"No," Stone admitted. "But I do have a good relationship with his Clan." Stone opened the door for her, and she preceded him into the darker interior of the restaurant's lobby.

She remembered then, that her grandmother had told her shifters had Tribes, Packs and Clans, and the word they used depended on their species and the size of the group. Werewolves travelled in Packs, so if Stone was referring to Peter's group as a Clan, then he probably wasn't a werewolf. Diana tried to imagine what sort of shifter Peter might be for a moment, but her inner conjecture was interrupted when the maitre d' saw Stone.

"Ah, Mr. Stone," the man enthused. "We

have your usual table ready and waiting. Please follow me, sir."

The welcome mat had definitely been rolled out for Stone, and Diana had the startling thought that maybe the entire staff of Alfredo's was made up of shifters. Could that be possible? One of the finest restaurants in town was operated by shapeshifters? Was the owner a shifter too? She was starting to believe that just about anything was possible where these creatures of magic and fur were concerned.

They were seated and given menus. The table had a strategic view of all the doors and was against a wall with no windows. She noted the way Stone just casually looked around every few minutes, as if checking the perimeter. Must be a wolf thing. Or an Alpha thing. Making sure everything was secure in his domain. She found it endearing rather than scary.

She looked at the menu, noting the lack of prices next to any of the entries and tried to think what would be the least costly of the items offered. She didn't want to order lobster and cost the poor man an arm and a leg. He'd already fixed her car for free, and she didn't feel right about any of it.

He wasn't being nice to her for sexual favors. She'd made it pretty clear last night that, if they'd been alone, she would have been incredibly easy for him. So, she didn't feel there was any quid pro quo expected or implied. He didn't have to fix her car or spend money on fancy meals to get her to jump into his bed with him.

No, he was doing these things because he wanted to. Not because he wanted something from her that he couldn't get in other ways. Hell, all he had to do was crook his little finger someplace where they could be alone, and she'd fall into his arms, no questions asked. He was just that potent, and she was just that smitten.

A terrible thought suddenly occurred and she put her menu down. "You don't have like, a girl in every port, do you?"

"Every port?" he looked confused.

"Like a sailor," she tried to explain. "I mean, you don't have a lot of girlfriends, do you? I'm not just one of many? I'll know if you lie. Tell me the truth."

"Did someone cheat on you, Red?" he asked, his eyes going suddenly fierce, as if he would tear the man limb from limb for hurting her.

"I'm not answering that until I hear your answer," she countered. It wouldn't do to be weak with this man. He was an Alpha. He'd walk all over her if she didn't stand up for herself once in a while.

He sat back and watched her from narrowed eyes, but relented. "I wouldn't be here with you if I was dating someone else. I wouldn't have done any of this if I was sleeping with another woman." His expression was still thunderous, but she felt the truth in his words. "I'm old enough to know what I want and not have my head turned by every pretty thing that walks by."

Something Oma had said about shifter longevity suddenly reared up in Diana's mind. "How old are you?"

"Older than you, Red. By a mile. Now, answer my question. Did some scumbag cheat on you?"

"Yes, but I'm not telling you when or who," she told him quietly, picking up her menu once more.

She thought she heard a growl from across the table but ignored him in favor of scanning the menu. "Don't they have just a plain salad?" she muttered to herself.

"Please tell me you're not a vegetarian."

Stone's tone sounded mildly horrified and made her look up at him.

"No. I'm a carnivore, but, um… I just want a salad." She tried to bury her nose in the menu again, but she caught the softening of his features.

"Honey, I can afford anything on this menu and then some. Get what you like. I insist." He pushed the top of her menu down gently with one finger, making her raise her gaze to meet his. "Do you like ribs? Maximo is a genius with ribs. He does great steak too. Or lobster. He's really just a genius in the kitchen, in general."

"Ribs are too messy for a first date," she replied, thinking aloud.

"Steak, then. How about filet mignon? He wraps the edge in bacon. You'll love it."

Filet mignon? That was always a pricey dish. She tried to demur, but the waiter came over at Stone's gesture, and he ordered for them before she could object. The only question she was left to answer was how well she wanted her meat cooked.

CHAPTER NINE

Stone had ordered a bottle of red wine to go with their meal, and the wine steward brought it over and uncorked the bottle with great ceremony. She was seeing Stone in a whole new light. He wasn't some uncultured mechanic. Oh, no. This man seemed totally at home with the traditions and manners of the upscale restaurant. She was the fish out of water here.

She wondered just how old Stone was. If shifters lived for hundreds of years, like Oma had said, he could've been raised in the more formal times of a century ago, or more. It boggled her mind, just thinking about it.

"Penny for your thoughts," he said after the wine guy left the table. Stone looked at her over the brim of his glass, and she felt her tummy flip. Had a more seductive man ever been born? She didn't think so.

"Just remembering a few of the things Oma told me about...um...your kind when I was little. This all feels very surreal, suddenly," she admitted, looking around the fancy place.

"It's real." He reached across the small table and put his hand over hers. The warmth of him made an impression and sent shivers up her arm. His magic tingled.

"I really don't understand what's going on here, or why this is all happening now, but thank you for bringing me here. The place is lovely."

"As is the company," he told her with a grin, releasing her hand and moving back as the waiter returned with a basket of piping hot bread.

Diana busied herself with a roll and the butter that was served with it for a few moments, trying to collect her thoughts and calm her pulse. Everything about this encounter was like something out of a romance novel. The handsome man. The fancy setting. His perfect manners and attentiveness. It was like a dream. A really good dream that she didn't ever want to wake from.

"Chef Maximo sends his compliments," the waiter said as he dropped off a plate of mixed appetizers.

"What's this?" Stone asked, a bemused smile on his face.

"Chef has been developing a few new appetizers, and he would like you to try them and give him some feedback," the waiter replied, then left them alone again.

Diana noted there were two of everything on the dish that had been placed between them. She used her bread plate to take one of each of the delicacies.

"This looks yummy," she said as she speared a roll of what looked like paper-thin eggplant and mozzarella dressed with crushed tomatoes and basil.

"I told you. He's a genius with food." Stone lifted a bite-sized ball of fried something off the plate and popped it directly into his mouth. An expression of enjoyment broke over his face as he chewed then swallowed. "You've got to try that. It's a shrimp ball or something. It's really good." He took his fork and pushed the remaining ball onto her plate.

They spent the next few minutes eating the little tidbits and comparing notes on flavors and favorites. They had surprisingly similar likes and dislikes, although neither of them disliked any of the offerings all that much. By the time she'd sampled half of the bite-sized morsels, she was mostly convinced Stone was right about the chef being a genius. Her taste buds were dancing with delight at each new flavor and texture.

Their lunch came just as the last appetizer disappeared, and the plates were rearranged by the waiter's expert hands. Diana found herself contemplating the most decadent filet mignon she'd ever seen. The edge was wrapped in thick, crispy bacon, just as Stone had said, and the whole thing was still sizzling. The aroma was divine, and even the vegetables on the plate had been presented with an eye toward perfection.

"This is almost too pretty to eat," she said, lifting her gaze to find Stone looking at her.

"It tastes even better than it looks," he assured her, lifting his own knife and fork in practiced fingers. "Dig in. You're going to love this."

She did as he suggested and found herself fighting a moan at the first bite. It wouldn't do to make such sounds in public, but her taste buds were in ecstasy. She met Stone's gaze as she chewed and swallowed, then shook her head.

"You were right. I've never had anything this good. I can see why everyone raves about this place."

They didn't speak much as they concentrated on their food for a few minutes, but it wasn't an uncomfortable silence. She paused a few times to sip her wine and comment on the vegetables and the way the dish was cooked and presented. Stone told her little details about the chef that intrigued her. He claimed Maximo was an old friend and a perfectionist who fussed over everything that came out of his kitchen.

From his words, Diana started imagining the chef to be a diminutive man who scolded all his helpers. The man that emerged from the kitchen was nothing like the image she'd built in her mind. No, Maximo was a huge bear of a man dressed head to toe in denim chef togs with his name embroidered on the upper left side of his chest in small, black letters. He was the total opposite of the white-clad fussbudget she'd been picturing, but he greeted Stone with a warm smile and outstretched hand.

"Alph—Mister Stone—so good to see you again." It was pretty obvious Maximo broke off the word Alpha the moment he got a good look at Diana. The two men shook hands, and the chef pulled a chair over from a nearby table and sat at the side of the table, so he could see them both. "Now, who is this lovely lady?"

Stone made the introductions. "Diana Pettigrew, this is Chef Maximo Alfredo. One of the Alfredos for which the restaurant is named. Max, this is Diana, a client and new friend."

"Any friend of Stone's..." Maximo let the sentence remain unfinished. "What did you think of the appetizers?"

They spent the next few minutes discussing each of the appetizer selections in detail. Diana found herself telling the man more than she'd thought she would, from her objection to slightly too much pepper in one of the sauces to her desire for a pinch more basil with the crushed tomatoes. She hadn't really thought he'd want such granular feedback, but he seemed truly pleased with her observations, so she got bolder as they conversation went on.

"Stone, you've finally brought me someone with a truly sophisticated palate," Maximo enthused as their conversation about the new items drew to an end.

The chef was all smiles, and Diana felt like he really meant his compliments and that he hadn't taken any of her criticisms the wrong way. Not that there'd been all that much to criticize. She was sure she'd given many more compliments than complaints.

"Tell me, Diana, do you cook?" Maximo asked unexpectedly.

"Well...for my grandmother, of course, but nothing so grand as what you've done here. I just cook the usual stuff, and I'm not professionally trained. I just learned from Oma," she admitted.

"Oma? You're German?" Maximo asked, his head tilted to one side in that almost animal way she'd noticed Stone sometimes had.

"Dutch," she corrected the man gently.

"She's from Holland."

"Ah. The land of wooden shoes and windmills. I spent a lovely few years in Amsterdam, once upon a time." Maximo seemed almost wistful. "We will talk more the next time you come," he decided. "And you must bring your oma along sometime. My Dutch is very rusty, but I might be able to remember a few words."

"You speak Dutch?" Stone asked before Diana could.

"I did once upon a time, but it was a long time ago," Maximo said, rising from the chair he'd appropriated. He turned it around and put it back at the other table with one hand. "And now, I must go and make sure the staff haven't moved all my knives while I've been out here. They like to play tricks on me like that sometimes." He winked and left the table, heading back to the kitchen.

The man was a bit of a whirlwind for someone so large. He wasn't fat. He was just...bulky. Built on the huge side—both tall and wide, but not around the middle. It was his shoulders that took up most of the room and gave an impression of a giant.

He looked like a bear. That thought sort of stopped her in her tracks. Maybe he was.

He'd been about to call Stone *Alpha*, which meant he was probably some kind of shifter. And heaven knew he was big enough to be a bear.

"They all keep wanting to call you Alpha," she remarked, trying to sound casual. "Then they see me and think better of it," she observed. "Are they all shifters?" she asked in the quietest tone she could manage.

Even so, every eye in the room turned to look at her with varying degrees of alarm or anger. They'd all heard her? Holy crap!

Stone stood up and held up both hands, palms outward. "It's okay. She knows, but she's cool. I'll explain it all to your Alpha, but this is Diana. Human, but with hereditary knowledge. Say hello, Diana," he directed toward her.

"Hi," she replied weakly, feeling a little sick at the idea that she was totally surrounded by people with what were probably lethal instincts and the claws to back them up. Crap.

Some hard looks were sent her way, but universally, those looks were transferred to Stone and eased. He was an Alpha werewolf, after all. He probably had a lot of status in this group, even if they had different animal spirits inside them. Still, Diana felt the somewhat uncomfortable regard of pretty much every person in the restaurant as they finished their meal.

"How about we take our dessert someplace a little quieter?" Stone asked, and she was more than ready to leave the restaurant—and the scrutiny of all those suspicions shifters—behind.

He escorted her to the door, where a shopping bag with the restaurant's logo on it sat waiting for them. He picked it up, nodded to the maitre d'. Diana and Stone went outside, where her old car was already waiting for them at the curb, the sandy-haired young man grinning as he held the door open for Diana to get in. She noticed Stone slide the kid a tip and another pat on the shoulder before he took his own seat on the passenger side.

She drove away, still conscious of eyes watching their progress. She figured every shifter in the place had probably been wondering what in the world Alpha Stone was doing with a human like her. Oh, he might say she had some kind of magical presence, but she knew it was all bull. She was as human as the next person. Nothing special to see here. She'd given up on ever developing a true magical gift long ago. Those were dreams she had well and truly put away for good.

But Stone… He was magic personified. She might be able to enjoy his company for a short time—and she was fine with that, or at least as fine as she could be with it—but for the long term, he would probably find a mate among his own kind. She *knew* that. She'd thought about it long and hard ever since finding out the truth about him. She'd thought she'd made her peace with the idea that she could only pass through his life, but not linger.

The looks she'd gotten on her way out of the restaurant, though, had made her feel distinctly uncomfortable. Like, why did a human even dare to go out with an Alpha werewolf? Like she was some sort of magical social climber, reaching too far above her station. Worse, she knew about them all being shifters, and she sensed more than a bit of hostility directed her way. Oma had always said that shifters held their secrets close and only shared the knowledge of who and what they really were with members of their own family, Tribe, Pack or Clan.

Very few humans knew that Others existed at all, and it had to stay that way, in order to protect them. Diana had considered the possible consequences of humanity learning that shapeshifters existed. She knew darn well that it wasn't a good idea to go blabbing about magic, or shifters, or any of the Others her grandmother claimed lived in secret among everyone else. Nothing good could come of such a revelation, and it could lead to war among the races and a great deal of strife. No way did Diana want to be even remotely responsible for that kind of thing.

"Make a right up here," Stone said, breaking into her racing thoughts.

"Where are we going?" she asked, glad to be alone with him and curious about where he was directing her to drive.

She wasn't nervous about being with him. Not by a long shot. Something deep inside made her trust this man where she wouldn't have been so easy to trust anyone else on such short acquaintance. She didn't know what it was, but she trusted her senses on this. She was a good judge of character and Stone was a steadfast sort of man. She felt it deep in her heart.

"We're actually headed to my place. I've got a great view of the desert off the back deck. It's one of my favorite places. Is that okay with you?"

His place? Hell, that was more than okay. They could be alone, and presumably, he had a bed somewhere in his house. Things were looking up. She might just get lucky this afternoon, after all.

She would've blushed at her own thoughts, but heat was already coursing through her system. The heat that lived just below her surface lately was up and running, urging her to go wild. To act with abandon. To...fly.

She didn't understand where any of those impulses were coming from. She couldn't fly, but somehow... No, she really didn't understand it.

But she could definitely do something about the urge to take a walk on the wild side. It didn't get much wilder than a sexy Alpha werewolf who was leading her back to his lair. *Growl*.

"Oh, that's fine. I love the desert. It's the whole reason we moved here. The heat is good for Oma's arthritis, and I felt really at home here when we came to see the place.

The desert calls to me," she admitted. "I'm not sure why."

CHAPTER TEN

Stone had his suspicions about exactly why the desert called to her. It remained to be seen whether or not he was right, but the more he was around her, the more familiar her latent power felt to him.

He'd spent years working for Lance when he'd been holding the phoenix inside. Diana's presence felt about the same. If and when her inner power broke free, Stone wanted to be there to help her deal with the fallout. He'd seen Lance go through the transition, and phoenix shifters had a much rougher time of it than any other shifter Stone was aware of. Most of them died.

In fact, Stone had been in touch with the Lords after Lance transitioned and had learned that his friend was the only known active surviving phoenix shifter in existence at the moment. The Lords of all Were tended to keep track of such things. At least, they tried to. A lot of their information was based on self-reporting, so it was possible there was another phoenix shifter out there somewhere that hadn't phoned home, but such enormous power was hard to hide.

In the weeks since Lance had transitioned, inquiries had come from all over. A human mage school had sent a representative to open negotiations for any feathers Lance might shed while in bird form. Apparently, such items had a potent magic of their own and could be used in spell work. Lance had sent the mage packing, even though the man had offered incredible amounts of money.

Lance had been adamant. His magic would only be used for good and only by those he'd personally checked out. If he shed a feather or two, they were to be collected and preserved until Lance found someone he trusted. He'd almost violently declared that he wasn't about to auction off parts of himself to the highest bidder. Stone respected that decision and had vowed to help his friend and the chosen Alpha of the Phoenix Clan—as they'd come to call themselves recently—protect the gifts of his animal form.

Before Lance had transitioned, he'd felt drawn to the desert too. Or so he'd told Stone after the fact. During the crucial period, Lance had pretty much kept his problems to himself. When he'd run into Tina again, that had seemed to be the event that pushed him over the edge into finally realizing his other half.

So, when Diana talked about the desert calling her, it was just one more piece of evidence in the case Stone was quickly building that pointed toward the likelihood that she was also a phoenix shifter on the verge of discovering her true self. Lance had been in touch with the Lords of all Were several times and had received visits from a priestess and her snowcat shifter mate who made their home in Las Vegas. Both had already been friendly with Tina, so their visit served more than one purpose.

They'd revealed the strange events happening all over the magical world that pointed to a buildup of the forces of Light. There were rumors that the Destroyer of Worlds had returned to the mortal realm, and the theory went that the forces of Light were gathering in greater numbers and stronger representations specifically to prepare for the confrontation ahead.

The priestess had offered up the idea that, if Lance's power hadn't been needed in this generation, it might very well have remained dormant for the rest of his human life. But something had sparked all kinds of happenings all over that made historians draw parallels to the last time the Destroyer had threatened the Light in this realm. There had been a buildup of power then, too. A half-dozen phoenixes had fought in that great war, using all their gifts to the best of their abilities.

Since that time, many centuries ago, phoenix shifters appeared only rarely and never more than one or two at a time. Now, however, it could be possible that more than one might awaken. Stone would lay odds that Diana would be the next to transition. He wanted to help her come through it safely. To return to Earth and not burn up in pursuit of the sun, only to be reborn into a new incarnation. No. He wanted her to survive in this form. To be…with him.

He didn't fully understand the impulses driving him, but they were stronger than any he'd had before. She couldn't fly to the sun to perish. Not his Diana. No, she belonged here. With him.

"I like the desert too," Stone admitted, trying to keep his tone casual. He didn't want to let her in on the severity of his thoughts. Not yet. "It has a character all its own."

He directed her to the turnoff that would take her to his home. He lived on Pack lands, near the rest of his people but set apart a bit to give him some privacy. The Pack house was nearby, and he could walk there in a few minutes or run there in his wolf form in about sixty seconds. He was close enough to be there for his Pack, yet far enough away to have a little room to breathe.

"We chose this place many years ago," he went on, talking about the land over which she was driving. "It was kind of a coincidence when Lance opened his shop not too far away. I went down to check him out and ended up with a job. As his business grew, more of my Pack started working there. Not everybody is a mechanic, of course, but enough of our younger Packmates enjoy tinkering with engines that there's always somebody interested in learning more through on-the-job training."

"So, your whole Pack lives around here too?" Diana asked, looking around at the desert vistas and the houses sprinkled here and there among the cactus.

"These are Pack lands. We own them as a whole, and each member is entitled to a place here, though if they want a new house, they have to build it," he replied.

"It's a communal set up? Sort of like an Indian tribe?"

He could see she was grappling with a way to understand how they lived and shared their property. She'd understand in time. Especially if she turned out to be who he suspected she was.

"Close, but not quite the same. Legally, because I'm Alpha of the Pack, I'm the owner of all this land. It's taxed as ranch land with dwellings and outbuildings for extended family and employees, but that's pretty far from the truth. We have barns we use as garages and workshops. We have a big Pack house where anyone can grab a meal or stay if they need temporary housing for whatever reason. We work together as a group for the good of the Pack."

"That sounds really nice," she said, smiling gently. "I like the idea of everyone helping one another."

"A Pack is built, first and foremost, on love. We are all family, whether related by blood or chosen. We take care of each other. We also will fight to the death for each other, and we're loyal—sometimes to a fault. That's part of being what we are." He would never have shared so much with a casual acquaintance, but the more he was around Diana, the more certain he became that she was someone very special indeed.

"That's really beautiful, and something I never really thought about. I mean, I knew shifters existed—at least, my grandmother claimed they did—but I hadn't really thought about how the wild instincts and relationships of the animal spirit must translate to the human side." Again, she favored him with an almost ethereal smile, as if she was charmed by the magic of what he was telling her.

His inner wolf was pleased by her easy acceptance of his words and the way he lived. He felt a little smug as he directed her to the gravel drive that led to his house.

"What was that big house we just passed?" she asked as she made the turn.

"The Pack house. Combination mess hall, hotel, meeting place, you name it. We use it for just about everything we do as a group, and there's someone there twenty-four-seven. If it's not the grannies playing cards or cooking up a storm, it's the youngest cubs playing together in daycare. And there's always someone living there for whatever reason. We have parties there at night, or community activities, and the kitchen is open for three meals, plus late night snacks."

He couldn't keep the pride out of his voice when he talked about his Pack and how well it functioned, but he figured he was entitled. He didn't have a huge Pack, but it was well run and had all the advantages he could devise for a Pack its size. They were growing, too. They'd taken in new members through mating, but more than one good-hearted lone wolf had been lured into the fold in recent years. He counted each one of

BIANCA D'ARC

those a small victory. Wolves weren't meant to be alone.

"I always thought Oma was exaggerating when she talked about shifters," Diana marveled, looking around at Stone's domain. "But a lot of what she said makes sense seeing all this and hearing about the way you live. She claimed that you all worked for the good of the collective and that your families extended well beyond what humans considered close relatives."

"A lot of it depends on the kind of shifter you're talking about, but what she said is pretty accurate," Stone told her. "Especially for wolves. We're long-lived compared to humans, so we tend to interact most with those we know are as long-lived as we are. Otherwise, it just gets depressing." He laughed to ease the truth of his words, but she gave him a sharp glance that said she understood what he was getting at.

She drove the rest of the way up to his home in silence, and he was sorry he'd let slip one of the harsh truths about being a magical creature with centuries to live. He hadn't meant to bring down the mood. Hopefully, eating whatever sweet treat Maximo had sent along would help restore

114

her cheerfulness.

Either that or he would have to kiss that worried look off her face. Hmm. Maybe a little of both. He wasn't making any assumptions about what would happen in the next hour or so, but he certainly hoped it would end with them together…naked. In bed. Or anywhere the mood happened to strike. He was flexible that way.

She parked her SUV in front of his house, and he jumped out and went around to help her out, even though it wasn't strictly necessary. Good manners never went out of style—or so his granny had told him—and he just wanted to be as close to Diana as he could get. She didn't seem to mind when he opened her door and helped her out from behind the wheel.

He grabbed the bag with the desserts and led the way to the front door of his home. He'd tidied up a bit before leaving this morning, in hopes he'd be able to convince her to come back with him after lunch. He was glad he'd done so now. First impressions were also important—another teaching of Granny's—and he didn't want her to think he was a slob. Women didn't like slobs, in his experience.

He opened the door and ushered her into his home. He hadn't had a human out here in a long time. He got the occasional visit from building inspectors when the Pack wanted to add on to *his ranch*, but he didn't usually entertain non-magic folk in his home.

CHAPTER ELEVEN

Diana's first impression of Stone's home was that it was a lot of space for one man. The house was built in a ranch style, with a great deal of genuine southwestern flair. Adobe, dark wood, tile. Cool surfaces under the hot sun. A single floor that spread out in all directions from the front door.

He ushered her inside and led the way through the enormous front room toward the back of the house. They stopped momentarily in a large—almost commercial-looking—kitchen, where Stone paused to open the bag from the restaurant. He found a tray in one of his cupboards and set out the boxes on it. There was also a bottle of wine in the bag, which Diana had not realized. Stone fetched two crystal glasses from another cabinet and asked if she didn't mind bringing the tray as he led them into another room with floor-to-ceiling windows that was both cool and inviting.

The entire house was kept much cooler than the outside temperature. Comfortable for a human and, she supposed, a werewolf, as well. There was a small table and two chairs in one corner of the room. They were at the rear of the house, overlooking what had to be miles and miles of open land.

"Is all this land yours?" she asked as she set the tray on the table and just looked out on the inviting vista for a moment.

"It's the Pack's," he reminded her. "I'm just the caretaker. I hold it as protector for the rest of my Pack."

"That's kind of a beautiful system," she said. "As long as the Alpha is a good guy."

He smiled as she sat in one of the comfy-looking chairs at the table. "A bad Alpha is soon replaced. Although, I will admit, sometimes it takes a while before that happens. Still, any dominant can challenge an Alpha. It's a mark of respect if an Alpha goes unchallenged for a length of time. It means his people are happy with him, and the Pack is stable. Alpha challenges happen a lot more often in unstable situations, and it can take a while to sort itself out."

"That sounds rough," she commented, trying to imagine what might constitute an unstable situation within the confines of the werewolf Pack.

"It can be. But that's also why we have a higher authority. Any Tribe, Pack or Clan can seek help from the Lords of the Were. They can step in and sort things out if things get really bad."

"I remember my grandmother mentioning Lords of some kind a long time ago, but she didn't have a lot of information." She smiled as he poured wine for them both then set about opening the containers holding two different kinds of cake.

"Keeping our secret is really important. Sure, other magical folk know we exist and we know they exist, but we don't go around talking about it to non-magic people. We all know the shitstorm that would rain down on us if humans knew we were living next door. I don't think the neighbors would take kindly to a werewolf Pack roaming nearby, do you?" She grimaced, and he went on. "The Lords are special, and we don't talk about them to just anybody. That your granny had even heard vaguely about them is interesting. We protect their secrets above all others because they have the good of all shifters at their core."

"I keep wondering why you're so freely telling me all this. I mean, I have no magic of my own." She sipped her wine and accepted the serving of cake he offered.

"That's just it. You do have magic. It's just...unfulfilled." His eyes squinted as if he was trying to figure out how to explain his thoughts. "I sense it all around you, and it feels really familiar, but I think it's waiting for something in order to come out."

She paused with a bite of cake on her fork. "You think it's going to manifest?"

Holy crap! He thought she was going to come into the magic that was part of her genetic heritage? She'd given up on ever having magic of her own, but maybe...just maybe...she'd been wrong. Maybe she was a late bloomer.

No. Couldn't be.

Could it?

Emotions rocketed back and forth in her mind. Having magic had been one of her deepest desires since she was a child. Stone made her hope again. But she worried that getting her hopes up would only lead to disappointment. Again.

"Being around you feels a lot like it did being around a friend of mine before his magic came out in a big way. There's a feeling of expectation. It sort of rubs against my fur and tingles when I'm around you," he explained. "Do you know if there's any shifter blood in your heritage?" he asked. He'd asked once before, but she hadn't known what to say. Maybe the time had come to reveal more of what she knew.

She shook her head. "Just some fanciful stories from way back. Oma always said some of our distant ancestors liked to exaggerate. We have diaries and journals going back almost a thousand years in the family archive."

Maybe she shouldn't have told him about the books. That was supposed to be a secret, of course, but he was trusting her with things he probably shouldn't have told her. And anyway, the archive was safely tucked away somewhere nobody would ever find it who didn't know where to look.

"Let me guess." Stone sent her a playful look. "Somebody way back when claimed to be a phoenix?"

"Is that the same as a firebird?" she asked, puzzled.

His grin grew wider. "I knew it."

"Wait a minute. Are you telling me that firebirds really do exist? You have a friend who is one?" She could hardly believe what his words implied. She'd thought it was all just colorful myth passed down through the centuries.

"I know of one," he told her, his expression now a tad guarded, even if he still looked more than a little triumphant. "And you feel just like he did before he changed for the first time."

She sat back in the chair, totally flummoxed. "I can't believe this."

"You probably should. I suspect your inner phoenix is just waiting for a nudge in the right direction, and when it flies for the first time, you're going to need to remember there are people down here who need you.

The temptation to fly to the sun will be very strong. You mustn't follow it. If you don't come back, you'll die and be reborn and have to start all over again, with a new life in a future time."

"Seriously?" She just looked at him. It was all a bit much to take in.

"That's what I've been told by people who have reason to know."

"Well, I would never leave Oma. She needs me, and I love her."

Diana thought about the call of the sun and the temptation of the heat of the desert. Would Oma's love be enough, though? Would that be sufficient to call her back from the warmth and Light? She hated that she wasn't sure.

"That's good," Stone told her, though his own expression said he wasn't altogether convinced that would be enough either.

"Oma let me read all about the gifts of the firebird when I was little, but I'm not sure I remember it all. There was something about her being able to see evil and burn it without burning anything else," she told him, trying to drag up those old memories of something she'd thought had just been a fantastical story.

"I've seen that first-hand. My phoenix friend can shoot flames that only burn evil. It's pretty amazing to behold."

She read complete honesty and a bit of admiration in Stone's gaze. He wasn't kidding. The fairytales she'd read about as a child were *real*. Oma would be tickled when Diana told her, but she wanted more information first. Especially since Stone thought Diana was going to grow wings and fly to the sun anytime now. Oh, dear. She just didn't see how *that* was going to work.

"The firebird who wrote our family chronicle lived for over five hundred years and probably would have lived a lot longer, but she was part of the forces of Light that fought against a great evil called the Destroyer of Worlds. Still, she claimed that her magic affected those around her, and everyone she loved lived longer than they probably should have, as well. She thought maybe the firebird herself was immortal, but that she could be killed. Her daughter wrote in a later entry that her mother had, indeed, been killed in battle with the servants of darkness." The memories of reading that ancient tome were coming back faster, now that she was talking about it. "So, the first two gifts of the firebird were being able to see and flame evil and being close to immortal. Then, there was the clairvoyance."

"That's attributed to the phoenix magic?" Stone asked, apparently surprised by her words.

"Apparently. Oma has a bit, as had several of my ancestors, if their chronicles are to be believed. Which is why I didn't totally dismiss the firebird's chronicle. There was just enough familiarity there to make me wonder if maybe she was just really good at embellishing," Diana admitted. "But if you say firebirds are real, then maybe everything she wrote was actually factual. I'm going to have to reread her chronicle at the earliest opportunity." She thought that last bit aloud then gnashed her teeth. "But this is all conjecture. I'm not a bird, nor have I ever felt the need to turn into one, no matter how much the desert and the sun call to me."

"If I'm right, you will shift eventually. Whether by choice or by necessity," Stone said in a grave tone as he regarded her steadily.

CHAPTER TWELVE

Stone decided to back off a bit. He'd scared her with talk of the mythological phoenix, which she knew as the firebird. They still had some time before she shifted—or so he hoped. He'd planted the seed. Maybe it was enough for now.

He refilled her wineglass then began to eat the decadent cake Maximo had sent them home with. He'd chosen the cheesecake when he saw the way Diana's eyes had lit up on seeing the triple chocolate delight that she hadn't yet touched.

"So, do you see the future?" he asked casually as he began eating his cake. He was trying to lighten the mood a bit and get her back onto firmer ground emotionally.

"Nope. Never have," she admitted and finally brought the forkful of cake to her mouth.

Her eyes went soft as she tasted the first bite, and he imagined naughty things about inspiring that sort of languid look on her face. She was a sexy little thing, and she lit a fire in the pit of his belly that would not be quenched.

"That's okay. I dabble," he assured her, teasing. "Like, I can foresee that you're gonna get kissed before this day is through."

"Oh, you see that, do you?" Her expression lightened, just as he'd hoped, and she jumped into the nonsensical banter with both feet. "Oma always gives me a peck on the cheek when I say goodnight to her."

"No, the kiss I foresee is way more intense than a peck on the cheek, and it's definitely not from your granny," he told her, knowing the wild desire she inspired was probably showing on his face, but she wasn't backing away.

She looked down though, unable to hold his gaze, and sipped at her wine, forestalling having to answer for a moment. When she looked up and met his gaze again, her cheeks were flushed just the tiniest bit. He found it utterly enchanting. How long had it been since he'd been with a woman who could still blush as the merest hint of his plans to kiss her?

More often than not, in recent years, sex had been gritty and needy, with someone who was just as worked up as he was. Usually another shifter who had to scratch the itch or have her wild half drive her mad. Those encounters had been fast and fleeting, over as soon as the urge had dissipated, but both parties had left happy and still friends. He just hadn't felt any sort of bond with those women, nice as they were to favor him with their bodies. And none of them had felt a bond toward him.

He'd know if they had. Shifters mated for life. When the bond formed, both parties felt it, and that was it. Mates. Forever.

"Do I get a say in this?" she asked, her voice dropping into an intimate whisper.

"You most certainly do," he replied, dropping his own tone down a bit, fostering the changed atmosphere between them.

She tilted her head a bit, considering him, then nodded gently. "All right then. I'll take it under advisement, but you know, even Oma's visions aren't always one hundred percent accurate. A lot depends on correct interpretation."

"Fascinating," he murmured, and he hoped she knew he was talking about more than just her words. He found this woman to be utterly beguiling, even when she wasn't trying to be anything of the sort.

He could almost feel her innate magic reaching out to him, twining around him, stroking his fur and caressing him. Warming him with her phoenix fire that didn't burn. He could only imagine what it would be like to bed her when she had come fully into her power. He wasn't quite sure he would survive, but it would be a hell of a way to go.

They ate their dessert as the sun began its slow descent across the desert. He noticed how she followed it, glancing at it every few moments from the corner of her eye, as if she couldn't help herself.

Maybe he could distract her a bit and get her to know him a little better at the same time. He'd pretty much decided that he wanted to get to know everything there was to know about her over the course of the past couple of hours. She fascinated him on every level, and he wanted to be there when she discovered her true power. He wanted that fulfillment for her, like he'd seen Lance come into his destiny.

Lance was his friend, and he'd been there for the guy, but Diana was...something different. Stone didn't just want to be there for her, he found he *needed* to be there. His wild side wanted to protect her, and his human side wanted to remind her of the joys of being here on Earth, and help her remember to come back and not die in fiery immolation.

That would just be tragic. And Stone didn't do tragedy. At least, not well.

"Do you want to meet my wolf?" he asked her as they finished the cake and lingered over the wine. She looked mellow as she watched the sun travel across the sky, and he was feeling a little frisky.

She looked at him, ripping her gaze from the sun's progress. "You have a pet wolf? Or do you mean...?"

"I mean... Me. In wolf form," he replied with a teasing grin. "Maybe watching my shift will help you discover your inner phoenix. At the very least it may help you not be apprehensive should you find yourself wanting to grow feathers and jump into the air."

"How did you know?" she asked, naked emotion in her expression.

"Wolf cubs start to shift at different times. Those whose wolves make them wait until puberty, or even later, start to get apprehensive about the entire process. First timers are notoriously nervous, especially if they haven't been exposed to the process enough. I have a current Pack member who grew up in a human orphanage, not knowing what he was. The first time he shifted, he was fifteen years old. It totally freaked him out, but he was lucky enough to come across a magic user who steered him in my direction. We sorted him out and helped him overcome his fears. I would like to help do the same for you, Diana." Every single word he spoke was the truth.

What he didn't tell her was how he felt *compelled* to help her. Driven by some higher force to show her the secret ways of shifters and help her come into her true power. She would be magnificent. He just knew it.

"That's kind of fascinating and scary, all at the same time," she told him.

He smiled and stood, moving a few feet away to disrobe. He had to admit, just to himself, that the idea of stripping in front of her turned him on in a way he'd never felt when stripping off with his Pack. Nakedness among shifters was a necessary thing. A simple matter of course. But being naked in front of Diana held an unexpectedly sensual component.

Was this what it was like to have a shifter mate? He didn't know because he'd never felt the mating bond with any of the shifter women he'd bedded. Just need. No time for subtlety. But he wanted to be all sorts of subtle with Diana.

"What are you doing?" she asked, her voice suddenly sounded a little strangled as his fingers started undoing his shirt buttons.

"If I shift in my clothes, I'll ruin them. Most clothing doesn't take kindly to the changing shape and size of my arms and legs, not to mention the different dimensions in different places. Almost all shifters have to physically take off our clothes if we don't own a sweat shop somewhere that can keep us in new shirts and pants twenty-four-seven." He chuckled as he pulled the tails of his shirt out of his waistband.

"What kinds of shifters don't have to...uh...undress?" she asked a little breathlessly, her eyes drifting around the room but still stealing glances at his progress. He noticed she wasn't watching the sun at all, anymore. Good.

"Well, it's only rumors, but they say the super magical shifters don't need to undress. Their clothes simply go someplace else and then come back when they resume their human form. Wolves are somewhat mid-range on the magical power scale, so we need to do things the old-fashioned way," he told her, tossing his shirt over the chair before starting on his pants.

He saw her swallow visibly then reach for her wineglass, and he had to smother a laugh. She was incredibly cute, this woman. Cute and classy, and with no real concept of the power she hid within. If it was up to him, he'd help her discover her true destiny. He wanted that for her. He wanted to see her at her full power. He had the notion that she'd be a true and just arbiter of the Goddess-given fire she carried in her soul.

"I remember now. Oma said that bears

were very magical," she said, her tone a bit squeakier than it had been before as he lowered his zipper.

"Yeah, they have a lot of concentrated power in their big, burly hides. But they still have to undress." He kicked off his shoes and socks, letting his pants rest, unzipped, just below his hips.

He didn't want to traumatize the lady, merely get her mind off the sun and onto the possibilities of being a shifter. Much as he wanted to wave his dick around at her, it probably wasn't the best strategy at the moment. She'd been raised human—albeit with a knowledge of magic—after all.

"As long as I make room for my tail, I can shift from this point without ruining my pants," he told her. "A bear couldn't do that. They have fat asses in their fur." He laughed, and she gave a slightly nervous answering titter. "Don't be scared now. I'm still me, no matter what outer shape I wear. I won't hurt you, no matter what. Okay?"

She nodded, seemingly lost for words as she watched him. Stone lowered his pants the strategic amount necessary then let the change come.

Magic buzzed around him, and he felt the

painful ecstasy of his body reforming into his other self. He went from standing on two feet to kicking away his useless pants with his hind legs. He hadn't taken time to pause in the in-between fighting form. He didn't see the need to unnecessarily scare Diana, and he knew that form was fearsome. Later, if she didn't run, he'd show her the advantages of the half-shift, but for now, he went straight to his furriest, fluffiest shape, hoping she liked what she saw.

CHAPTER THIRTEEN

Diana felt the magic buzz across her senses, but she didn't feel threatened. It felt...comfortable. Familiar, somehow.

She'd never been especially sensitive, though she knew the basics of magic. Oma had prepared her, in case she grew into her power as she aged, but that day had never come, though she'd retained all the arcane knowledge usually reserved for magic users. By rights, she probably shouldn't know half the things she did, but she was glad for it.

Knowing what Stone was made him somewhat less scary, though when he finally sat on his haunches before her in his wolf form, she found her nerves zinging in her body. He was enormous! Bigger than any dog. Bigger than any wolf she'd ever seen on the internet. He was absolutely massive. And fierce.

And he had his tongue lolling out the side of his mouth like a big goof. She smiled at him, and he seemed to take it as an invitation to move closer. He padded up to her chair slowly then stopped right in front of her, looking at her with those cunning eyes.

She could still see him in there. She could see the sparkling intelligence of the man she'd spent the afternoon with. He might be in wolf form, but now that she'd witnessed this, she knew she would never mistake a shifter for its animal form. He might be in the shape of a wolf—an enormously huge wolf—but he didn't *feel* like a wolf to her, if that made any sense.

Oh, he had the animal wildness, but it was tempered by a keen human intelligence. She thought she finally understood how shifters could be both animal and man—something she'd never quite grasped before.

He tilted his head to the side as if to ask, *"Well?"*

"This is…pretty impressive," she told him. "I didn't expect you to be so large in your wolf form," she went on, not sure how to express her thoughts and how much she could say without sounding foolish.

Not being able to talk with him was a definite drawback of the animal form, she quickly realized. She'd never had a pet. The apartments and condos she'd lived in with her grandmother hadn't allowed them. So, she'd never really gotten into the habit of keeping up one-sided conversations with animals. She supposed there was always time to learn.

He moved closer, putting his large head over her knee. Surprised, she raised her hand, not sure what to do next.

"Do you want me to scratch behind your ears?" she half-joked. When he nodded his head vigorously then rested his jaw on her lap, she laughed outright. "You realize this would be really weird if you were still in human form," she told him, reaching behind his pointy ear and scratching lightly.

His fur was so soft. She hadn't expected that. She sank her fingers into his lush pelt and almost gasped. The sensual thrill of touching him sent a little thrill from her fingers, straight down her spine. She suppressed a shiver as best she could, but he seemed to know. His eyes twinkled, and his tongue reached out to lick her resting hand.

"This just gets weirder and weirder," she murmured, but didn't pull back. There was something strangely sensual about the entire encounter, which would be obscene if he was really just a wolf, but knowing the man was in there… Well, it changed everything.

She was hyper aware of his head on her lap. His eyes remained watchful, taking in her every reaction. He saw too much, probably. More than she was really comfortable revealing on such short acquaintance. But then again, everything about their brief relationship was vastly different from anything she'd ever experienced.

Everything was new and different with Adam Stone. Everything was…really confusing.

He lifted his head from her lap suddenly and turned to look out over the desert. Had he heard something? Could he see something she didn't? She figured that was likely.

Suddenly, a howl rose from the desert. A wolf howl.

He padded closer to the window and raised his head, letting loose a howl that must've carried to the other wolf. It sure was loud in the confines of the room. More wolf voices joined in unexpectedly from outside, and Diana realized they were sort of surrounded by what had to be werewolves.

She probably should have realized they would be. They were on what he called Pack lands, and he was their Alpha. His people lived all around here.

The wolf song tugged at something deep inside. Some primal part of her she hadn't yet realized was there. The complex harmonies told a story that was just out of reach but that fascinated all the same.

It went on for a few minutes then faded away in the distance. The Alpha had added his voice to his Pack's, here and there, loud and long, but not uncomfortable. Sure, she'd never been around a vocalizing wolf before, but somehow, it felt...right. Familiar, if she could use that word for something she'd never participated in before.

She didn't understand it. But then, she'd

had experiences in her life before that she didn't fully understand but accepted. Oma's clairvoyance. The very occasional knowledge that came to Diana when she was in the presence of magic. It wasn't reliable, and it wasn't often, but every once in a while...

Yeah, freaky things happened sometimes. Only...they didn't really freak her out.

She supposed that was due to Oma's teachings. Or, maybe, there was some dormant part of her that knew and accepted things that would give a normal person nightmares. Maybe that latent bit of her that Stone—amazingly—claimed might soon come to fruition knew all was well with the world...even the freaky bits.

She still felt a bit off-kilter from the wave of magic that had washed over her when he'd shifted. So much so that she felt lightheaded suddenly. She closed her eyes and felt the room spin. Something inside her wanted out, but she didn't understand how. It was frustrating—and incredibly dizzying.

She felt her body sway in her seat and everything went blank for a moment.

The next thing she knew, a wet tongue was licking her face. A dog? She didn't have a dog.

No. Not a dog. A wolf. The Alpha wolf. Adam Stone.

She'd been in the back room of his house, having a meal. Then, he'd shifted, and she'd seen his wolf form. Then she'd swayed…and then… She must have blacked out.

Yet, he was still in his wolf form, so it couldn't have been for long. Diana shook her head to clear the cobwebs and pushed the wolfy nose away gently.

"I'm okay. It's all right. Just give me a moment." She sat back in the chair and kept her eyes closed, trying to calm the racing of her heart and the tangle of her mind.

A second wave of magic came at her, and this time, it had the effect of helping calm her. It was as if the first wave—when he'd shifted to wolf form—had rubbed her feathers the wrong way. This new magic settled them back down in the right positions.

Feathers? What the hell?

Was she really buying into his claim that she was going to shift into a firebird?

She thought about that for a moment and realized she was. That part of her that had always longed for magic was alive and kicking and wanting more than anything for his wild claims to be true. She wanted to be a firebird, like her ancestor before her. She wanted to be a shifter.

That was kind of new. Always before, she'd wished for magic like her great-grandmother or her mother, who had died too young to grow fully into her power. But according to Oma, Diana's mother had been born with great potential and was casting spells even before she'd hit her teens. Then she'd met a man and had fallen in love. They'd married young and had a baby—Diana—and then, they'd died. Tragically. Accidentally. Much too young.

Leaving Diana with her grandmother.

Her thoughts of the past were interrupted by the sound of fabric and the metallic clank of a belt buckle. She still didn't want to open her eyes, but it sounded like Stone was being chivalrous and putting on his pants before he came back over to her. She could feel his energy now, moving across the space to join her once again. It was funny how she was now hyper-aware of his movements. It was as if a sixth sense where he was concerned had been awakened, and she wondered idly if she would always be this aware of him from now on.

143

"Are you okay?"

His deep voice came from nearby. Was he kneeling at the side of her chair? She pried open her eyelids. Yes. Yes, he was.

"I just got really dizzy. I think I blacked out for a moment."

She shut her eyelids again, against the visual stimuli that hurt her eyes. For some reason, everything was shining and golden. Especially Stone. He was outlined in shiny gold and green. What the heck?

"If you did, it was only for a split second," he told her.

She was glad to hear it. From the way she'd felt when she'd come back—as if she'd been gone a long time and a great distance— she was reassured to hear it had been a lot quicker than it had felt. She decided to level with him. Maybe he knew more about what had just happened. He seemed to have a lot of arcane knowledge that she didn't. Maybe the blacking out and the funky vision was a shifter thing.

"It felt a lot longer," she admitted. "And when I open my eyes now, everything's shiny. You have a gold-green glow around you."

"I do?" He seemed surprised. Hmm.

Maybe he didn't know what was up with her, after all.

"Yeah." She nodded.

"Some people can see auras," he offered in a contemplative tone. "Many priestesses have that gift, from what I understand. And shifters generally see in the way of their animals when in shifted form. I have a problem with color perception in wolf form, but things don't exactly glow. I wonder if…" She heard him move slightly, then she heard the sound of a cell phone being used. "I'm going to call on an expert. Hold on a minute, okay, Diana?"

"Yeah. I'll be right here," she told him, feeling tired all of a sudden. "No problem."

She heard the call connect as Stone moved away from her. His voice was a low murmur that was somehow soothing to her senses, though she couldn't understand what he said to the person on the other end of the call.

A few minutes later, he was back. "Do you see everything in shades of gold, red and orange, or just living things?" he asked out of the blue.

"I'm not sure," she replied, curious as to what that might mean.

145

"Try it. Open one eyelid and look around," he coaxed her.

Taking a deep breath, she did as he asked. One eyelid, then two opened. It wasn't as painful this time, but it was disorienting. Stone was a huge gold-green presence in front of her, but as she let her eyes adjust, she realized the only certain things in the room were glowing. Him. The plants scattered all around. Everything else was just there. Normal. Not glowing.

She turned to the big windows and looked outside. The desert crawled with glowing life, but the sand was just…sand. And now, she could see moving spots of warm color moving—no, loping—along in the distance. Wolves. Running and walking. Near and far. Shifters in the wilderness she hadn't been able to see before.

There were a lot of them.

"I see wolves," she told him. "Bright golden wolves. And insects. Red and yellow and golden brown. And plants. Green-gold plants. But the rest is normal."

"Did you hear that?"

She looked up at him, but he was clearly talking to the person who was still on the other end of the phone. He nodded a few times and made agreement sounds, then ended the call with thanks and farewells.

"He says it sounds very familiar. That's how he sees when he's the phoenix."

CHAPTER FOURTEEN

"Do you really believe I'm going to become…" She couldn't even finish the sentence.

Her hands were trembling, and something inside her suddenly couldn't cope. She shut her eyes again, this time against tears.

Whether they were tears of fear or of joy, even she wasn't sure.

"Hey, hey now." Stone was at her side again, taking her shaking hands in his.

He was closer this time than he'd been

before, kneeling at the side of her chair. He put one arm around her shoulders, and she couldn't help herself. She leaned into his strength.

She felt like she was coming apart at the seams, but he was solid. Sure. Safe. He seemed so confident that he knew what was going on. Maybe he did. Maybe she really was turning into a bird...shifter. It sounded so insane, but she knew, deep in her heart, that it wasn't.

"Shh." He crooned to her as he took her into his arms, comforting her.

How long they stayed there, she didn't know, but she welcomed it when he stood, taking her up into his strong arms. He carried her straight to the wide couch she'd seen in passing before, when she'd entered. He sat down, keeping her on his lap, cuddling her close.

He felt so good, and not just in the physical sense. She sensed his innate goodness now. It was as if the change to her vision had changed a lot more about her, as well. Her senses were operating on a whole new level.

She chanced opening her eyes again, and was met with a much more mundane scene than before. There were still glowing spots here and there—plants and the occasional spider—but she felt better able to deal with it now. The desert, and seeing the wolf Pack roaming there, had been overwhelming. This plainer scene was a bit easier to take.

Of course, Stone was still the brightest light in view, but his aura—if that's what it was she was seeing—was pure and bright. Comforting. Good to the core.

If she'd had any doubts about him before, they were shattered now that she could see the goodness shining out of him. No way could anyone fake that sort of Light. She believed she was seeing the Light of his soul, and it was untainted by any darkness.

Yes. He was definitely one of the good guys, and she found that both calming…and incredibly sexy.

"Hey, you're looking at me," he said in a gentle voice as he looked downward to meet her gaze. "You feeling better now?"

"A little. You're still all golden, but it's not as blinding now. It's easier in here where there's not as many things that are alive," she admitted.

"Maybe you just need time to adjust," he murmured, leaning close to place a gentle kiss on her brow.

The move touched her deeply. It was a sign of care that went far beyond the few hours of their acquaintance. But things Oma had told Diana about shifter mating came back to her. She'd always thought the idea that they knew their mates almost on sight was incredibly romantic.

Then again, she'd felt a near-instant connection with Stone. If she truly was a shifter, would she recognize her mate so quickly? And if so, could Stone be the one? The one being in all the universe meant solely for her?

Suddenly, she wanted that. She wanted *him*. Forever.

She wasn't sure about anything anymore, but she knew she wanted more than just a few kisses and a cuddle. No. She wanted to know what it felt like to be Stone's lover. She'd wanted that from almost the first moment they'd met, and if she had anything to say about it, she wouldn't let another sun set before she took him into her body. The memory of his lovemaking into her soul.

Decision made, she lifted her head, meeting his intense gaze. "Make love to me," she whispered, being bolder than she ever had before.

"What?" His eyes widened then took on a dazed, hopeful expression.

"You heard me. I have a few more hours before duty calls me back. I want to spend them with you. Naked. In bed. Or on this couch." She looked around, a smile touching her lips. "Wherever."

"Seriously?" He drew her gaze back to his by placing both hands on her cheeks and gently turning her face. His touch was so careful. As if he cherished her already. As if he was afraid to harm her in any way.

"I'm very serious about this, Adam." She used his first name deliberately, trying it on for size. If she was going to take him into her body, she sure as hell was going to call him by his first name.

He'd said nobody called him Adam, which was perfect as far as she was concerned. It would be her special name for him. An intimacy shared.

She could actually see the spark of desire light in his eyes this time. Her new vision was something entirely different but very useful in evaluating what was really going on with the living beings around her. She couldn't think of a better person to learn about her new talents with than Adam Stone. He was both wild and gentle, and she wanted to experience everything he had to offer.

He swallowed hard and then leaned his forehead against hers. "I want you to know that I'm serious too." His voice had deepened, taking on the growl of his wolf side. She found it utterly compelling in the sexiest possible way. "I knew you were special when you walked onto the car lot. That's why I've been hounding you."

She smiled. "You're a werewolf. Can you *hound* people?"

He smiled back, and it lit her world. "I wanted to know everything about you," he admitted, moving in for a quick peck on the lips. "That's why I prowled around your condo last night. I never expected to get caught at it." He kissed her again, with a little more pressure.

"Oma's pretty sharp. She saw you. Or, should I say, she foresaw you. It's hard to get anything past her when she's got visions coming in." This time, Diana reached out to touch her lips to his, darting her tongue along the seam of his lips until he let her in.

The kiss lasted considerably longer as she wound her arms around his neck. He hadn't

BIANCA D'ARC

put his shirt back on. Just the pants, which were only buttoned and zipped. The belt hadn't been fastened. And his feet were bare. He probably hadn't taken time to put on his underwear either. Hot damn. He was going commando.

She moved one of her hands to his chest, wanting to learn the feel of him, but he broke the kiss and stood from the couch with her still in his arms. The sheer strength of the man nearly stole her breath.

"Where are we going?" she asked as he began walking, carrying her as if she weighed no more than a feather.

"I liked your first choice for location," he told her with a wicked grin. "Let's try the bed first, then we can explore other options."

Stone could hardly believe he had her in his arms and was taking her to his bedroom. They'd only met the day before, but in his heart, he knew without doubt. She was the one. The mate he'd waited all his life to find.

More powerful than he'd expected, she was a phoenix shifter who hadn't yet shifted. It was a dangerous time for her—and for him. If she shifted before their bond was

154

formed, he could very well lose her to the sun. She would fly away and die. Burning up, only to be reborn. But her next incarnation wouldn't be his mate. He would live his life alone and lonely if he lost her.

He had to do all in his power to bind her to him now, before she shifted. Maybe the mating bond would be strong enough to call her back when she made her first flight. He had to believe it would work. For without her, his life would be empty. Devoid of joy. And love.

He carried her into his bedroom and laid her gently on the bed. He had never taken a woman to this room. If he slept overnight with a female, it was usually in her territory. In her bed. This room he'd kept as his inner sanctum ever since he'd finished building the house. It was the one place in his life where no one intruded.

He belonged to the Pack everywhere else, but this house—and especially this room— was his private place, where he went to unwind and just be Adam for a little while. He liked that she had called him by his first name. Nobody did nowadays. Not since his folks had left this realm. It felt right that Diana call him that. A name just for the two of them.

Her eyes were filled with the flame of the stars—or one star in particular—but he didn't tell her. She would change soon, but before that, he had to make her his in every way possible. It was almost a race against time. A race against the sun and its claim on her. He had to claim a part of her heart first, before he could let her answer that call to the sun. Only then might he have a chance of her returning back to Earth. To him.

It was a risk, but there was no other choice left to them. Lance had come back and continued to return to his mate. Stone needed Diana to return to him...for the rest of their lives.

He stood at the side of the bed and unzipped his pants, letting them drop to the floor. Then, he joined her on the bed, moving gently to her side, trying not to startle her.

He shouldn't have worried, though. When he got close enough, her little hands were all over him, as if she was as hungry to touch him as he was for her. Damn, that felt good. She touched him as if...as if she truly cared.

Love was something outside his

experience with sex. He hadn't dated human women, even in his youth, knowing they were all too apt to fall in love with him. A love which he couldn't reciprocate. He'd always known his mate would be a shifter. A shaman had told him so long ago. He'd limited his partners to shifter females ever since, knowing the unions were born of need. Not love.

Not until now.

That's when it hit him. If she was his mate, then this time would be about love. A first for him.

He almost laughed. At his age and experience, Diana was making everything new. Who'd have ever thought it possible? Certainly not him.

When her hands left him, he grew concerned. Had he done something wrong? He broke off the kiss that had filled his mind with steam and realized she was tugging at the little black dress she had worn to lunch. A hot little number, she'd looked good enough to eat.

Which reminded him…

Stone took her hands in his, stilling them as he slid down her body. He settled between her knees, liking the way she

157

shivered when he showed a little bit of dominance. He'd have to explore that later, but for now, he had other things in mind.

Settling her hands on his shoulders, he used his own to push the hem of her dress higher. She'd worn stockings, but he was amazed to find that they were actual stockings—with sexy black garters and little bows. Frilly underwear he hadn't expected, but that set his body burning.

"Oh, honey. Did you think of me when you put these on this morning?" He lifted his gaze to meet her eyes, and the shy smile she sent him confirmed his suspicions even before she answered.

"Do you like it?"

"Like it?" He had to chuckle. "If I liked it any more, this would already be over before it got going. Of course, I recover fast, so you wouldn't have to wait long before I could show you how much I adore what you did to prepare for our lunch date. Do you have any other surprises for me to uncover?"

"Unwrap your present and find out," she taunted him, surprising him again, with her boldness. Damn. His woman was frisky. He liked that.

"I like the way you think," he told her,

returning his attention to her uncovered legs.

He could just see the tops of her creamy thighs above the sheer black stockings. He pushed the stretchy fabric of her dress higher to uncover the elastic strings of the garter and the matching frilly black panties she wore underneath. His mouth went dry when he saw the bows on the side.

"They untie," she told him unnecessarily.

Holy shit. She'd come dressed for seduction. If he'd known she was wearing this get up under the relatively conservative dress, he wouldn't have made it through lunch without coming in his pants. Repeatedly.

He needed to see more before he unwrapped that particular present. He wanted her to explode first, then he would join her. Especially this first time, he wanted to show her how it would be if they spent their lives together. He would always put her welfare, her pleasure, her needs, above his own. Always.

He was going to prove that to her now, and every day they were blessed to be together from here on out. He prayed silently that they would be many, but he wasn't taking anything for granted. He needed to show her how much he cared for her. How much he needed her. How he burned for her.

He had to make her burn for him.

And then, maybe, when she went up in flames surrounded by her phoenix fire, she would remember the man who could make her burn without dying in the sun. Maybe she'd remember...and come back to him.

Impatient now, he pushed the dress higher and uncovered a shapely waist. His fingers trailed over her skin, raising goose flesh wherever he touched. She was responsive to him. Good.

Satisfaction filled him as he pushed the clingy dress over her breasts, revealing the black bra that matched the set below. Fuck. He had never seen anything sexier.

He pushed the dress up over her head, removing it completely so he could see all of her in the sexy black lingerie she had chosen to wear for him. Humbled by the thought that she'd already made up her mind—at least on some level—that if the opportunity presented itself, she'd be ready for him to claim her, he lowered his lips to hers.

CHAPTER FIFTEEN

His kiss was gentler than she'd expected. Almost reverent. She'd wanted to drive him wild, but instead, she seemed to have touched him on some other level. A deeper level, if she could believe the feelings she could sense coming off him in waves.

Care. Surprise. Appreciation. A feeling of being deeply moved.

She hadn't expected that. She figured he'd be horny when he saw her undies. Instead, he was touched. She wasn't sure what it meant, but his reaction touched her, as well.

What had started out as wild need had morphed into something almost...sacred?

He moved over her, blanketing her in his warmth as the kiss deepened. She felt the heat of his body over hers, and she wanted more. So much more.

His big hands played over her skin, tugging the cups of her bra downward to reveal eager nipples. His mouth left hers, but she didn't mind as he traced a wet path with his tongue down her neck and then over her chest. He sucked at her nipples, laving them just the right way to drive her insane with desire.

All the while, she felt his fingers playing with the little bows she'd tied on her bikini panties. How she wanted them gone! But he was making her wait. Making *them* wait. And it was a delicious sort of torture that she truly didn't mind. Not really.

Then, the first little ribbon came loose. Sweet heaven, he was finally getting to the good stuff. First the right side and then the left, the panties came untied, and he swept them away, suddenly impatient.

His mouth became voracious on her skin as he worked his way downward. He paused at her bellybutton then moved lower, spreading her legs wide as he lay between them.

And then, he was there. She could feel his hot breath playing over her most sensitive place. She hadn't been with all that many men in her life, and none had ever gone down on her before, but she'd fantasized.

She'd fantasized a great deal. She just never expected this to happen so fast, but she'd prepared in every way for her big lunch date, including doing a little extra trimming and shaving. She was as ready as she could be for this...unexpected as it was.

"You don't have to..." she mumbled when the pause extended beyond her comfort zone. Was he having second thoughts? Was he really not as into this as she'd thought? A million possibilities went through her mind as the moment stretched.

"Are you kidding?" He looked up, meeting her gaze, and the sheer image of him lying there, between her splayed thighs, his hands possessively grasping her legs as if to position them just where he wanted them... Well... That image would probably stay with her for the rest of her life as the hottest thing she'd ever seen. "I'm savoring, sweetheart. Give me this moment to appreciate you."

Oh. When he put it that way, she got all shivery with anticipation, again. Damn. The man could turn her on like a switch.

"Just don't take too long," she whispered, feeling bold again.

He nodded slowly. "Your wish is my command," he said, moving one hand so that it touched her spread lower lips, playing in the moisture that had gathered. Sliding. Teasing. Taunting... Entering.

Oh, yeah. Moving deep within on one long glide. It was only his finger, but she clenched around him, anticipating what would come when he slid his hard cock into her eager channel. She moaned, unable to form coherent words as he slid in and out again, then back in. He chuckled.

"Eager little thing, aren't you, Red?"

The golden glow around him intensified, but she was getting used to her new way of seeing. The glow was just around him, like a halo now. She could see him clearly, just with the added outline of the aura—if that's what it was she was seeing.

She couldn't answer his question in words, so she just made a humming sound as his hand toyed with her, driving her passion higher than she believed possible. Then, his mouth opened over her clit, and her hips wanted to rocket off the bed in stunned fulfillment as a climax broke over her. It was a small climax, and it didn't taper off, but built again, into an even higher state of arousal.

His tongue played expertly with her clit, making her whimper with inexpressible desire. He seemed to understand all the same. Then, his mouth closed over her little nub, his teeth playing gently over the slight distention, making her jump in surprised delight. She'd never felt anything like this before.

All the while, his finger fucked her, slowly. Steadily. Making her want more. And more.

She came again, and again the passion regrouped quickly and sent her into an even higher state of anticipation. What was this magic he had about him? Were all shifters so sexually gifted? If so, their mates were truly blessed.

As she regrouped from the most recent climax, he removed his hand and mouth, repositioning himself. She was disappointed for only a moment until she realized his intent. Finally. He showed her the goods she'd only glimpsed up to now.

Just as she'd thought. A thick, long, hard cock, eager and ready for joining. Claiming. Imprinting.

Once he took her, she doubted she'd ever be the same again, but that was all right with her. So much had happened since she'd met him the day before. She wasn't the same person, even now. It only made sense to see the transformation through to its conclusion. What she would be after this, only the Mother of All knew, but Diana trusted Her enough to hope the caterpillar would become a gloriously fulfilled butterfly.

"You're mine, Diana. Just so you know. There's no going back now." He paused, positioning himself at her entrance to meet her gaze. His tone was possessive, his expression serious. It drove her to look for words, though he'd driven most of them from her mind with his sexual skill.

"Take me. I am yours," she managed, agreeing with his claim, proud of herself for coming up with four whole words when her mind was in the torpor of passionate chaos. They must've been the right words because he smiled triumphantly and drove his shaft home, up into her willing core.

Yes! He was so big and so warm. It took her a few moments to adjust, and he gave them to her, holding still, his cock engulfed by her body, claiming him as he claimed her. It was a beautiful moment, but not meant to last.

As soon as she grew almost used to his size and girth, he began to move.

What followed was the wildest ride of her life. Fast, then slow, then fast again, in varying patterns, Stone rode her through peak after peak and still drove her higher. When the ultimate crisis came, he waited for her to crest the wave before joining her, shouting her name as he stiffened, his face rigid with the pleasure she had enjoyed over and over. At his hands.

She was feeling it again, her body thrumming happily as he finally joined her in bliss. She held onto him, loving the feel of his strong shoulders under her hands. Never had she been with such a man. Such a considerate lover. Such a skilled seducer of the senses.

Never had she felt the instant connection she felt with Adam Stone. Her Adam.

Now…and forever?

Oh, man. She had it bad.

But he'd been so forceful before. Saying she was his in that tone of voice that made her insides all wiggly. Maybe he was feeling as possessive of her as she was of him, but doubts rose in her mind, even as he turned them on their sides and cuddled her close.

"You're amazing, Diana," he whispered, kissing her temple as he spooned her against him.

She'd never felt so cherished in all her life. No man she'd been with before had wanted to just hold her afterwards. Not like this. This man was so damned special, it brought a tear to her eye that, thankfully, he couldn't see from his position behind her.

"You're not so bad yourself," she replied, keeping the emotion from her voice as best she could.

He seemed to hear it anyway. He turned her in his arms to look into her eyes.

"What is it? Did I hurt you?" He seemed genuinely concerned.

"Are you kidding. No, of course you didn't hurt me. It was wonderful. Best I've ever had," she told him.

His expression lightened as he smiled.

"Best ever, huh?"

She swatted his arm. "Don't let it go to your head," she told him, able to laugh now too. He was such an amazing man. How did she get so lucky as to catch his eye? And how long would she be able to keep it?

"Don't go broody on my, love," he said, his smile fading as he cupped her cheek. "Tell me what has you troubled."

"Nothing," she lied quickly, but his brows lowered as his expression grew stormy.

She realized something. "Hey, I don't see the glow around you anymore."

She looked again, seeing only his handsome face and glowering eyes. She saw the spark of his magic deep within, but the glow that had started out as blinding had faded to just a faint outline now. Thank heavens.

"Your body is adapting to your new senses," he told her. "That's good. But it also means that you're closer to shifting than I realized. I didn't expect your magic to manifest so soon." He reached out and kissed her lips tenderly. "I wanted to be closer to you before you shifted for the first time. I wanted you to be sure of your place here."

"In your house?" She sent him a confused look. He touched her, and her mind went on vacation, it seemed.

"In my life," he corrected gently. "I want you in my life, now and forever, Little Red. Didn't your granny tell you anything about shifter mating?"

"She said that shifters knew almost right away who their mates were when they met. Are you saying—?"

"You're my mate." He cut her off with the most amazing declaration she'd never expected to hear. And in her heart, an answering clamor rose.

"I think you're my mate too," she told him in a quiet voice, watching his beautiful, smoldering brown gaze to see his reaction.

Heat flared in his eyes. Heat and magic and the power of the Light. Yes. This man— this beautiful werewolf—was meant to be hers. She could feel it deep in her soul.

And wonder of wonders, he seemed to feel it too. Praise be the Mother of All.

CHAPTER SIXTEEN

They lay in bed together the rest of the afternoon, making love again, and solidifying the fragile new bonds between them. Stone continued to show her new heights to which he could drive her passion, and for her part, Diana began to tingle in every part of her being. It was a gentle buzz at first, but as they lay together in the aftermath of the best sex she'd ever had, she started to feel distinctly strange.

Her vision flared again, into the shiny

171

energy patterns, but this time, it wasn't painful. Maybe she was getting used to it?

Unable to stay still any longer, she got up and padded into the en suite bathroom. She splashed cold water on her face and cleaned up a bit in other ways, but it didn't help. The itch under her skin grew wilder, and fire started licking through her veins. Outside the small window in the bathroom, she could see that it was much later in the day than she'd thought. The sun was riding low on the horizon, sunset truly coming on in all its glory, painting the desert in reds, golds and oranges.

"Everything all right?" Her lover's voice came to her as if from far away, but she registered the warmth of his presence behind her as she stood, transfixed, at the window.

"I need…" She shook her head and tried again. "I need to be out there," she told him. "I need to feel the last rays of this day's sun on my feathers."

Feathers? Had she really just said feathers? And did she even realize what she'd just said?
Damn.

"Okay, love," Stone crooned to her, lifting her in his arms and walking as fast as he could to the back of the house and the door that would lead...either to a beautiful destiny...or his deepest despair.

He pushed the handle downward with the edge of his hand and kicked the door open. Then, they were outside, in the heat of the dying day. Hopefully, that would be the only thing dying tonight.

Stone sensed her crisis was near. Whatever the trigger, her phoenix wanted out, and he sensed it was about to show itself in a big way. He only prayed their new bonds were strong enough to bring her back once she'd tasted the freedom of flight.

Stone set her on her feet on the patio behind his house. He liked to sleep out here in his wolf form sometimes, so the area was tiled and kept neat. She'd be okay barefoot, as long as she stayed to the patio area.

She wore only his discarded shirt, which she'd thrown on when she'd headed for the bathroom. He'd liked that little show of modesty. And he liked even more that she'd covered herself with his scent. That meant something special to shifters. Especially wolves.

"The sun is setting," she whispered, leaning back against him as he looped his arms loosely around her waist.

They were both facing the setting sun. She was watching it, as if the brightness of its rays could do her no harm. Stone was watching her, knowing she held his future in her hands. All would be decided within minutes, he reckoned.

"You want to chase it, don't you?" he asked, knowing he'd never voiced a more important, or difficult, question.

Slowly, she nodded. "It calls me."

He released her and moved around to stand in front of her, momentarily blocking her view of the setting sun. He had to get through to her before she took off. He might never see her again after, and if so, he wanted her to know… So much. Too much to say in such a short moment out of time.

But he had to try.

"This is a big step, love," he said quietly, holding her gaze. He could see flames leaping in the depths of her eyes, and he knew she was close to becoming what she had always been meant to be. "Just please remember that I'm waiting here, on the ground, for you. I want you to come back. No. I *need* you to come back. My life would be forever incomplete without you."

Water filled her eyes for a short moment but was quickly burned off. "I feel the same about you, Adam," she whispered. "But I really have to...do...something...right now."

As he watched, her entire body clenched, as if in pain. He knew first timers had a hard time shifting sometimes. It was up to him to show her the way.

He kissed her forehead and let her go completely. "Watch me, Diana. Let go and come with me as I let the animal spirit take control for a moment. Don't fight it."

He stepped a short distance away, still holding her gaze and let the wolf come. He was already naked. He hadn't bothered to dress after rising from the messy bed.

He let the magic take hold of him and felt an answering rise in hot, phoenix-flavored magic coming from Diana. Stone let the wolf take him, but he stopped in the half-shift battle form when it looked like Diana was having a hard time giving over control of her body.

"Let go, Diana. Let the firebird merge with you," he advised, his voice tinged with the rough rumble of his wolf in half-shifted form.

That seemed to do the trick. The phoenix energy burst free in a blinding flash. Stone had to look away, and when he was able to look back, the woman was gone. The firebird trailed streamers of bright orange fire as her talons clattered against the tile of his back patio. Then, she launched herself into the sky.

Stone let the wolf take complete control, finishing his shift and raced after her as fast as his four legs could carry him. He was Alpha. He was swift. But she was born to fly, and she sped toward the setting sun, chasing it around the world. Halfway across Pack territory, Stone stopped running, allowing himself to trot more easily on a dirt road that only Pack members used to get to some of the more remote homes in their territory.

Fearing the worst, Stone stopped and sat, howling for his mate, praying for her return.

The freedom was amazing! She was flying. She was really flying! And the sun was taunting her, sinking on the horizon, daring her to chase it. She flew as fast as her magical feathers would take her, guessing she might look like a bright orange streak across the sky to anyone who could see magic.

But she didn't care. All that mattered was the sun. It was leaving her behind. Running away relentlessly while she chased behind. She had to catch it! She had to catch up.

Nothing mattered but her race with the sun. She wanted so much to bask in its warmth, to join with it and burn in its fiery flames.

Then, she heard a wolf howl in the distance. Faint, but unmistakable. It sounded so sad. So wounded.

What? Her human mind was puzzled.

The wolf was sad. She wanted to go back and comfort it. To tell him she'd never leave him behind. But the sun…

The firebird wanted the flames, but Diana decided that her firebird half was a bit on the nutcase side. Burning up in the sun? Forget that nonsense. The sun would rise again tomorrow, and she'd see it then. For now, Adam was sad and she suspected she was the cause of his upset. She had to fix that. She had to fix her mate. Her human side and her newly discovered animal spirit agreed. The mate was paramount. His happiness was more important than her own.

Wheeling in the sky as if she'd been born to fly, Diana retraced her path, back toward her waiting wolf.

She found him, not where she'd left him, but on a dusty road miles from the tiled patio from which she'd arisen. It didn't matter. All that mattered was that he was howling in pain, and she knew, in her heart, she caused it. She had to make it right.

Circling down from above, she spiraled closer to her mate. She hadn't realized she'd climbed quite so high. Were there any limits to how high the firebird could fly? She'd have to test that later, but for now, she wanted the Earth beneath her feet and her mate in her arms.

She realized quickly that he'd run after her. He'd covered all that distance on his wolf paws. He must be really fast to have made it so far in what had been only a few minutes. Or was it hours? No. Minutes. The sun wasn't down completely yet. It may have felt like longer, but it was only about fifteen or twenty minutes in the mundane world.

Good. She'd hate to think she'd prolonged her mate's unhappiness.

She wanted to call out to him but didn't quite know how. She opened her beak and a trilling whistle came out, unlike anything she'd ever heard before. Adam must've heard it though, because he looked up suddenly, pinpointing her progress as she spiraled down over him, getting closer and closer.

His howling ceased, and he rose to all four feet then shifted in a burst of golden-green magic to his two-footed human form. He stood there, tears making tracks down either side of his face that he didn't bother to hide. Gloriously naked. Watching her.

Oh, my. When the Mother of All picked a mate for someone, She sure knew what she was doing. There could be no more handsome man in all the universe. No more caring and thoughtful a partner to share her life with. No other for Diana, but Adam. Her man. Her mate.

She wasn't sure how to land, but she trusted the firebird to know what to do as she spread her wings in a final glide. She set her talons down on the dusty dirt road, a few feet away from him. He was smiling, and she wanted to be human again, so she could run into his arms, but she wasn't sure how.

"Don't over-think it, my love. Just let the animal spirit take a backseat and let the human part of you take over. You know what to do on an instinctual level." He coached her gently as she tried to do as he suggested.

After a moment of effort, she gave up trying and just let it happen. A few seconds later, she felt the magic break over her like a wave, and then, she was standing—not on talons, but on her own two feet.

And she was naked. Well, there was nobody out here but the two of them, so she supposed it didn't matter, but...

"How in the world are we going to get back to your house?"

He started laughing, and she followed suit as he pulled her into his arms, embracing her as if he would never let go. Joy and laughter united them as did the bond between their souls that had come into being that afternoon. Just in time.

"I heard you call me back," she whispered when the laughter faded and they were just standing there, hugging.

Her cheek was pressed to his chest, against the reassuring rhythm of his heart, and one of his arms was around her waist, while he stroked her hair with the other hand, his chin resting gently on top of her head. They fit together perfectly. As if made for each other. Which she was now convinced, they had been.

"I've never been so afraid in my life that you wouldn't hear me and wouldn't ever return," he told her, bare emotion filling his deep voice.

"As long as you breathe, Adam, I will always return to you." She leaned back a bit to look into his eyes. "I love you."

"You do?" His expression seemed hopeful, which filled her with the same emotion. "I mean, I figured, in time… But I already feel it, so I guess it's possible you do too."

"Feel *what*, exactly?" She favored him with a squint that teasingly told him of her impatience to hear the words back.

"I love you too, Diana. I didn't know it could happen so fast, but then, I've never found my mate before. I love you more than life itself, and I'm not sure I would have survived had you chosen to follow the sun."

Well. He couldn't speak much plainer than that. She rewarded him with a kiss, moving both arms up to tangle her fingers in the short hair at the nape of his neck.

CHAPTER SEVENTEEN

How long they stood there, kissing as the sun sank below the horizon, she didn't know, but the wash of headlights broke them apart some time later. A vehicle was heading toward them at a very slow rate of speed.

Only then did she realize there were golden-green haloed beings gathered all around them. Wolves sitting in a circle, around their Alpha...and Diana. Suddenly, being naked seemed a bit more embarrassing. She clung to Adam so the only thing everyone could see was her behind.

"It's okay," he crooned to her, whispering into her ear. "They heard my howl and came to find out what was wrong. I bet they've figured it out already, but we'll have a formal announcement at the Pack house as soon as you and I figure out logistics. You're the Alpha female now, as my mate. These are your people too. This is your Pack now as well, Diana."

"It's a lot to take in. And I'm not really comfortable with public nudity yet. Maybe I'll never be. I never thought much about it before." She raised her gaze to his, hoping he saw the humor in this that she did.

His broad smile was answer enough. "You've had a big day. Lots of changes. It's okay. We'll take this one giant step at a time, okay?" The vehicle had stopped a few yards away, and Diana heard a door open. Adam looked over at the big cab of the pickup truck and spoke to the driver. "Hey, Zeke, you got a blanket in your truck? My lady is learning all about her wild side today, but we're going to take it slow."

A minute later, an older man came over and draped a woolen saddle blanket over her shoulders. He looked at her kindly and smiled. She liked the man almost instantly.

"Shifting is always a little tricky the first time, but you'll get the hang of it," he told her gently, turning the edges of the blanket over to Adam's care. "Welcome to the Pack." The older man tipped his cowboy hat at her and stepped back as she smiled her thanks.

Adam wrapped the blanket around her the rest of the way and stepped back. He looked at the gathered wolves. "Everyone, this is my mate, Diana."

A joyous howl lifted to the sky from the throats of a dozen or more wolves. Answering echoes sounded from farther away, and Diana felt tears gather at the beauty of the welcome. She felt the magic of their song. It vibrated through her body as she realized the enormity of what had happened to her.

Not only was she now a shifter—a firebird, like in the legends of her family—but she had gained a mate and a Pack. All in the space of a day or two. She wasn't sure what all this would mean for the life she had led up to this point, but Diana knew Adam was fully aware of her commitment to her grandmother. Oma would be brought into the fold, too. Diana was certain of it, though she didn't know exactly how it was all going to work out, just yet. That had to be part of the *logistics* Adam had wanted to talk about.

"Zeke will give us a ride back to our place," Adam said as the howls began to fade. "We'll see you all later at the Pack house. Tell everyone. We're having a party," he told the gathered wolves. As soon as they heard that, they got up and ran off, scattering to all points to do their Alpha's bidding.

Only Zeke and his enormous pickup remained. He opened the door for Diana as Adam helped her up into the rear compartment of the crew cab. Adam followed her in, sitting in the back with her while Zeke retook his seat in the front and started the engine.

The ride home was easy. Zeke and Adam talked quietly while Diana closed her eyes. Her vision had stabilized, but she was starting to feel the stress of her exertions. She'd never flown before, and her arms and torso felt a little sore. It amazed her to think that the muscles she'd used as a bird had somehow shifted back to human and still retained a bit of soreness from the unaccustomed activity. That was kind of cool and weird all at the same time.

Adam's arm remained around her as she snuggled against his side, and somewhere between the dirt road and the gravel driveway in front of his house, she must've dozed. The next thing she knew, he was lifting her out of the truck, blanket and all.

Stone carried her into the house, across the threshold, which he thought was fitting considering human traditions. She was his mate. His bride, so to speak, though they hadn't had the official human ceremony yet. It was traditional to carry one's bride across the threshold. He smiled as he kicked the door shut.

"First, I'm drawing you a bath," he told her, wanting to pamper his mate to show her how much he cherished her. "You're probably a little sore from using your muscles differently. That happens a bit in the beginning."

"For wolves too?" she asked sleepily, seeming content to let him carry her through the house.

"For all shifters, I think," he told her as he made his way to the bathroom. "The magic of shifting heals a lot, otherwise we'd be a lot sorer after running for miles or, in your case, flying for the first time. But the shifting magic doesn't do it all. How do your arms feel?"

She made a little face. "You're right. They ache a bit. And the muscles all along my sides, too."

He bent to kiss her forehead gently. "A warm bath will help with that."

Sitting on the closed toilet lid keeping her in his lap, he reached over and started the water flowing into the tub. He rubbed her shoulders a bit as they waited for the tub to fill. She looked so adorably tuckered out. He just wanted to care for her and make her spark again.

Tossing the blanket aside to return to Zeke later, Stone lowered her gently into the half-filled tub. Then he went to the medicine cabinet and found the Epsom salts. He added a generous helping to the water and swirled his fingers around to help it mix.

"How's the temperature?" he asked. Her eyes were shut, her head resting against the rim of the tub.

"Perfect." The word was a whisper of happy sound.

"Try not to fall asleep," he told her, chuckling. "I'll come back in twenty minutes to see how you're doing, okay?"

A satisfied mumble was her only response. He still had the smile on his face when he left the bathroom, taking Zeke's blanket with him. He dropped the blanket in the living room on his way to the kitchen. Once she stopped being sore, Diana was probably going to realize she was hungry. Shifting used a lot of calories.

He opened the fridge and started pulling things out. Then he picked up his phone and made a call he hadn't been sure he was ever going to be able to make. He was calling his friend—his Alpha—Lance.

"How is she?" Lance asked without even saying hello when he picked up the phone.

"A little sore. She's in the bath," Stone told him.

"I saw her come back," Lance admitted. "Is she yours?"

"Yeah. She's my mate." Stone found himself choking up a bit at the admission he'd always hoped to make, but had never been sure was in his future. "We're having a little party at the Pack house later. Can you come?"

"Wouldn't miss it for the world," Lance told him. "I'm really happy for you, man."

"Thanks." Yeah, the emotion rising in his heart made it hard to express himself, but he knew Lance understood. Lance had found his mate a while back and Stone had never seen his friend happier.

Ending that call a minute later, Stone made some quick sandwiches, which would keep until Diana was ready. He also had some meat ready to grill, but he'd wait to put it on until he was able to watch it. Right now, he had a mate to check on.

He found her just emerging from the cooling water. When she sensed his presence, she looked up, charming him all over again. His mate was the most beautiful woman in the world. Truly.

He plucked a big towel off the rack and opened it, walking toward her. She stepped into his embrace, allowing him to enfold her in his arms, wrapping her in the oversized towel at the same time. Rubbing lightly, he dried her arms, delivering a light massage at the same time.

"How are you feeling?" he asked, lowering his head to kiss her temple.

"Hungry!" she told him, laughing at her

own words. "I feel like I could eat half of Texas right now."

"I made a plate of sandwiches, but I've got meat ready to grill," he revealed, eliciting a hungry rumble from the direction of her belly.

She pushed back and clutched the towel with one hand, using the other to push against his chest. "What are you doing here? Go grill that meat! I'll join you as soon as I've dressed."

He laughed at her urgency. "Impatient much?"

He teased her, but he understood. Shifting used a lot of energy. He was always hungry when he came back from a long run in his fur. He could only imagine what it was like for someone to fly halfway to California and back again.

He left the bathroom, still chuckling. He had his marching orders. Food. And plenty of it.

Diana found him in the kitchen. Her nose was sending signals to her growling stomach that told her a good meal was only moments away. Thank goodness. Who knew flying would make a gal so hungry?

"That smells amazing," she said, moving to his side at the stove.

The meat was already on a platter, grilled to perfection, but he was fussing with some smaller pots on the stove, with what looked like side dishes. Vegetables and some kind of pasta dish. Apparently her man could cook. This mate thing just got better and better.

She sat down and he brought things to her. She almost lost track of how much she'd consumed, but eventually, she felt a little less like a starving carnivore and more like a human being again. He didn't say much during her feeding frenzy, but the few times she looked at him, he had an almost goofy, indulgent expression on his face as he kept her supplied with food and non-alcoholic things to drink. Juice, mostly, which tasted sweeter than it ever had for some reason.

Everything tasted better, when she slowed down enough to actually taste what she was consuming. She wasn't sure whether to attribute the increase in flavor to his cooking skills or to the changes that were still taking place to her body. Her vision had been first, and very obvious, but what if even her taste buds were becoming more sensitive?

"How are you doing?" he asked, sitting at the table, eating one bite of his steak to every two of hers. She consoled herself by noticing the bite-sized morsels on his fork were almost twice as big as the ones she'd cut for herself. She wasn't a glutton or anything. She was just *hungry*.

Although, the raw feelings had left and she was starting to calm down. As if her metabolism was slowly starting to stabilize. The enormity of what had happened to her hit and she realized suddenly it was after dark.

"Where's my purse?" she asked, verging on panic. Her grandmother would be worried. It was way past the time she'd expected to be home.

Adam reached back with one arm, stretching to the counter behind him, then returned with the little black purse that matched her dress in hand. He gave it to her with no comment. He probably realized why she was freaking out. He knew darn well Oma was dependant on her for a great deal.

Pushing her plate toward the center of the table to make room, she reached into the purse and pulled out her phone. No missed calls. That could be either good or bad.

Either Oma was okay and didn't need anything or she had gotten into trouble and didn't have her phone nearby to call Diana. She hit speed dial for her grandmother's number, praying hard.

It was picked up on the first ring and Diana felt an instant relief.

"Oma, are you okay?"

"I think that's my question for you, pumpkin," came her grandmother's spry voice over the phone. "Something big happened. Are you all right?"

"I'm fine now. Oma... I... um... The firebird? It's real." Diana held her breath waiting for her grandmother's reaction.

"*Och*. I always told you she was real. You're the one who insisted it must be some made up story. She was as real as you or I. Now, are you saying this because you saw one or are you saying it because you *are* one?"

"The second." Diana shook her head. She should've known. Her grandmother was always a few steps ahead of her when it came to magical stuff.

CHAPTER EIGHTEEN

"Oh, my *liefde schot*, you've reclaimed the family birthright. I'm so happy for you!" Oma sounded more invigorated than she had in years. "I had a hard time interpreting what I saw for you. Flames. Lots and lots of flames. Which could have been a really bad thing, but considering our heritage, could have meant something else altogether."

"Why didn't you tell me?" Diana asked gently.

"And worry you? No. Not when I

couldn't be certain what the flames meant. It might have hindered you from the transition and I know better than anyone to not mess with Fate."

Diana decided to let that go and turn to more practical matters. "Are you settled? Do you need help with anything?"

"I'm better than I have been in years," Oma insisted. "I see a party in your future and it looks like that handsome wolf is glued to your side throughout."

"Uh... That's the other thing. Adam is...um...my mate."

"Well, no wonder he's staying so close to you. That boy is in love!" Oma laughed outright, with what sounded like pure joy. "I'm so happy for you. Now the other part of the vision makes sense. Tell your Adam to send someone around here to get me. I'm coming to your mating party."

Diana noticed Adam reach for his own phone. Could he hear both sides of this conversation? She thought about werewolf senses and realized he probably could. That would take some getting used to.

"Seriously?" Diana was taken aback. Her grandmother was old and unable to get around well. She never ventured out after dark and usually went to bed early.

"Perfectly. You know, something about what happened today affected more than just you. I feel ten years younger already and I suspect the changes haven't stopped yet." Her grandmother paused for a moment. "Remember the second gift of the firebird?"

"Longevity for all those she loved," Diana supplied, remembering the ancient chronicles of her firebird ancestor. Suddenly the implications hit her. "Do you mean...?"

"I think so," her grandmother replied. "Which means it could happen for all those in your inner circle. Your mate, any kids you may have, the extended family."

"The Pack?" Diana's eyes widened as Adam's gaze met hers.

"Is it a big Pack?" Oma asked.

"I haven't met them all yet, but yes, there are a lot of them."

"Shifters are already long-lived, but your presence will probably have an influence on them," Oma theorized. Adam tilted his head, clearly curious. "But you'll see what I mean when I get there. Send a car, since you have ours. Otherwise, I'd drive myself, I feel so good!"

Diana was nonplussed. What in the world

had gotten into her grandmother? Was the second gift of the firebird manifesting in everyone she loved? If so, what were the implications for Adam and his Pack?

"Now, go and get ready. I'm putting on my dancing shoes," Oma said into the stunned silence. Then she chuckled. "See you when I get there." Oma disconnected the call without waiting for a response.

Diana lowered the phone. "I can't believe this."

"She sounds good," Adam said with a casual shrug, revealing he'd heard the other side of her call. "I'm going to send Zeke. He's a bit older than her and he can give her a first-hand report on how you did on your first shift."

"When you say *a bit older*, how much is that?" she wanted to know, her mind still stuck on the idea that shifters lived longer than humans and her newfound firebird magic might have an influence.

"Zeke?" Adam seemed to consider. "I think he's about two hundred and fifty, give or take a few decades. I've never asked him."

That stopped her in her tracks. "How old are you?"

He looked both amused and a bit

chagrinned. "Honey, I've been Alpha of this Pack for about sixty years already."

"You're a centenarian, aren't you?" she asked, feeling really out of her depth. "Adam, I'm only thirty!"

"And now, you're the next best thing to immortal, so really, what does age matter?" He tried the charm, but her mind was exploding.

She had taken everything else that had happened today reasonably well, but this was the last straw. The enormity of the change in her circumstances was something that was going to take time to come to terms with. And her grandmother! She'd sounded so strange on the phone. So young!

Diana shook her head. Then she lifted her hands and rested her face in her palms for a moment. This was going to take some adjustment.

*

Stone arranged everything. Zeke was only too happy to go get Diana's granny. That old wolf had been single a long time and older magical women weren't thick on the ground. Stone suspected Zeke wanted to check out the new lady in the extended Pack first, before any of the other older bachelors got a chance. It was a wolf's nature…to never give up looking for that perfect mate.

Stone knew he'd waited a long time to find his mate. He hesitated to tell Diana exactly how old he was until she had a little time to assimilate all the changes. She had a rough idea. He had seen his century mark a while back. He hadn't denied it. But he'd wait for a bit before telling the exact date of his birth.

When she was calmer, he escorted her out of the house and drove her over to the Pack house, where the party was already in full swing. Wolves knew how to enjoy life and when there was a reason for celebration, they partied. A cheer went up when Stone walked in with Diana on his arm. Everyone was happy for the Alpha to have finally found his true mate—and such a powerful being at that.

Sure, there had been a few women in the Pack that had hoped to catch his eye, but wolves knew when they were meant to be and there were no hard feelings that the mating bond hadn't formed. It just meant that the search would continue. Wolves were tenacious when they were on the hunt.

The Pack was familiar with phoenix shifters now that Lance had transitioned. Many of the guys worked for Lance at the car lot and they universally respected him—and his new power. Lance had saved most of their lives during a pitched battle a few months back. He'd displayed the awesome power of the phoenix and his mate was something to behold as well.

Tina was a witch with a chilling sort of power. She was ice and her mate was fire incarnate. Together, they were the perfect balance of power, and the perfect overall Alpha pair to rule over a mismatched group of shifters that had gathered to Lance's power—even when they hadn't really understood what it was about the supposedly human shop owner that attracted shifters of every shape and size.

Stone had accepted Lance's authority over him and his Pack at the shop long ago, but now that Lance's power had been realized, Stone and his people had fully joined the Phoenix Clan, which was an amalgamation of Tribes, Packs and Clans under the Phoenix Alpha. The name was clever because outsiders would have no clue the Clan was named for the phoenix shifter at its head and not the city they all lived in or near.

And now, there were two phoenix shifters in the Clan. Stone wasn't sure how that might affect the power structure, but it shouldn't be too bad. He'd already been Lance's right-hand man. Now, with the addition of Diana at Stone's side, that position could only solidify. And, as she learned more and grew into her power, she might find herself a new role in the overall Clan as well. Stone would enjoy watching Diana learn about her abilities and how to use them for the good of both their Pack and their Clan.

Everyone wanted to see Diana and congratulate her on her first flight, as well as her mating to the Alpha. Normally, the wolves probably would've been a bit more grabby—hugging Diana like a stuffed toy—but she wasn't a wolf and the only experience they'd had with phoenix shifters was Lance and he wasn't exactly a hugger.

When Zeke showed up with Diana's granny on his arm, the room went silent. It was clear, this older woman was someone important, but few knew exactly what was going on until Diana ran to meet her grandmother near the door. She flew straight into her grandmother's arms and burst into tears.

More than a few of the maternal females shed a tear themselves at the display of raw emotion. It was clear, seeing them together, that they were related. Diana was a younger version of the older woman and Stone realized his Pack had needed to see this. The depth of Diana's love for her family was clear and it spoke volumes to a Pack that was built on bonds of love and family. This one moment did more for her acceptance in the Pack than she realized.

"Everyone," Stone said into the quiet that had fallen. "Let me announce this officially and introduce you to our new Pack members." Diana separated from her grandmother at his words, but kept one arm around her waist, standing at her side.

Stone walked over to the two women. Hetty winked at him, and her smile sparkled with life. She looked quite a bit different from the last time they'd met. Something had definitely changed her. Magic sparked against his senses—a sort of benevolent warmth tinged with age and affection.

Granny magic, if there was such a thing.

"My friends, this is Diana Pettigrew. Most of you saw her streaking toward California earlier tonight on wings of fire. She's a phoenix, or as her family knows it, a firebird." A howling cheer went up from the Pack, all gathered around, but it was clear he hadn't quite finished yet, they settled down to let him get on with it. "And this lovely lady, is Diana's grandmother, Hetty van Dunk. She sees the future, so be warned," he said with a smile, returning Hetty's wink.

He took Diana's hand and drew her away from Hetty with a soft smile. Hetty let her go, a happy expression on her lined face. He didn't take her far.

He kept hold of her hand as he went down on one knee. "You thought you were mortal until tonight, when everything changed, Diana," he said for all the Pack to hear. The hushed silence told him they were all listening. "Now, you're something else, but I want to do this by the traditions you were raised with. Diana Pettigrew, you're already my mate, but will you also be my bride?"

CHAPTER NINETEEN

"Yes." Tears rolled down her cheeks as Diana nodded. She bent to embrace him, and Adam stood, taking her into his arms and kissing her like they were the only two people in the universe.

For that moment out of time, they were.

Then she became conscious of the cheering and stomping, making the Pack house reverberate with laughter and joy. The werewolf Pack was gathered around them, and Oma was only a few feet away. Diana broke off from kissing him, a blush heating her cheeks, which only caused even more howling cheers and laughter from the assembly.

She heard a number of loud pops from one corner of the room and then glassed filled with bubbly champagne were being handed out through the crowd. Someone brought glasses to Diana and Adam, as well as her grandmother and then Zeke proposed a toast to honor Diana and Adam's mating. Everybody drank and cheered again and the party was truly started.

Someone had music going in another room and when Diana had a chance to peek in that doorway, she saw the younger crowd had an area cleared for a dance floor. They were celebrating in their own way, working off happy energy by jumping and moving to the beat. The older members of the Pack were seated around the edges of the big room and food was being passed around.

Everybody seemed to want to stop and talk with Diana and Adam. He remained firmly at her side, even when she turned to see where her grandmother had gone. She needn't have worried. Zeke had taken her to one of the side tables and was providing a plate of finger food and some non-alcoholic drinks for her. Oma was on several drugs and it wouldn't be wise to drink alcohol while they were still in her system. Whether she'd still need them now that magic had come into their lives, Diana had no idea.

"Do shifters and other magical folk have special doctors?" she asked Adam when she had a moment between meeting people.

"Healers," he replied. "We have a Pack healer who actually is an M.D., not that he needed that to deal with us, but it keeps the government happy. We have to live within the legal framework set up by the humans, so we send some of our folks to get the necessary credentials. We have a number of registered nurses in the Pack as well. Some even work in the profession at local hospitals and nursing homes. Why?"

She gestured toward her grandmother. "Oma will probably need some reevaluation. She's on a dozen different drugs and if the magic is changing her..."

"Don't worry about it. I'll get our doc to take a look at her first thing in the morning. He can handle any paperwork or prescription changes. You'll also need to change doctors. Heaven knows what your kind of magic will do to their instruments now."

He chuckled and she admitted there was probably something to his words. She'd miss her old doctor, but she couldn't risk exposing the changes in her physical form to a non-magical person. She had always understood the need for secrecy. It had been drilled into her from a young age. Especially after she'd been granted access to the family chronicles.

Come to think of it, she had better start writing a chronicle of her own now that she had some magic. It would help later generations if she made note of the things that had happened to her and the things she learned along the way. Oma had a journal, in which she made notes about her gift of clairvoyance, but since Diana had never manifested magic, she'd never had anything to contribute. Well, that had just changed in a big way.

The front door opened again and new murmurs went through the crowd, which opened up a direct line from where Adam and Diana were standing to the newcomers. An intensely magical couple were standing near the door if Diana's new vision proved accurate. The man...burned red and orange. And the woman was haloed in icy white.

"Come on. I want to introduce you to some great folks," Adam told her, reaching for her hand as they began walking toward the doorway. He stopped them in front of the newly arrived couple.

"Lance, Tina, this is Diana, my mate," Adam said into the hush that had fallen as everyone watched what transpired.

"And another phoenix," Tina said with a wide grin. "It's really great to meet you, Diana." She held out her hand and the two women exchanged greetings, sparks of magic filling the air as their magic met for the first time. "Cool," Tina said, watching the display with an infectious smile. "That's never happened before."

"What is it?" Diana whispered for all to hear.

"Fire and ice," Tina said, her tone contemplative and amused. "We spark off each other a bit. I didn't hurt you, did I?" Tina asked, suddenly contrite. "Sorry."

"No harm done. I didn't even feel anything," Diana assured her and Tina relaxed again.

"I'm Lance," the man standing next to

Tina held out a hand and Diana shook it. The feeling this time was one of warmth and...recognition?

"You're like me," Diana whispered, knowing the man was also a firebird shifter. A phoenix, as Adam called it.

Lance nodded. "I'm a newcomer to this whole thing too," he admitted. "But yeah, I'm a phoenix shifter. Nice to not be the only one around."

"I wonder if we're related somehow?" Diana asked, thinking aloud. Lance had a certain look about him that was somehow familiar. He looked a bit like her uncle had.

"We'll probably never know," Lance told her, his expression tightening as the handshake ended. "I'm an orphan. I grew up in foster homes."

Diana's heart went out to the man. "I'm sorry. But you look..." Diana shook her head. "My parents died when I was very young, but you look a lot like photos I've seen of my uncle. My mother's brother," she clarified. "They all died in a wreck—my parents and my uncle. He was driving and a semi came out of nowhere and crashed into them."

"I have no information on either of my

parents. Just that my mother died in childbirth at a local hospital here in Phoenix and nobody came forward. I was put into care and stayed a ward of the state until I was eighteen," Lance told her, reciting the story quietly, as if he'd come to terms with his origins a long time ago.

"Let me see him," Oma's voice came from just behind Diana. She whirled to find Oma barreling toward them under her own steam, Zeke following behind as every eye in the room focused on the little tableau by the front door.

Oma went right past Diana and walked directly up to Lance, putting one hand out as if to touch him, but she stopped short. Her eyes closed and Diana knew her grandmother was reading Lance's energy.

"You are one of ours," Oma said, her eyes popping open. "You are Gustav's child." Tears flowed from Oma's eyes now as she looked up at the tall man who looked a lot like photos Diana had seen of her Uncle Gustav, Oma's only son. "How is this possible? How did I not see it?"

"I'm sorry, ma'am," Lance said, a tight expression on his face. "I'm not really sure what you're talking about." Diana saw Tina reach out to take hold of her mate's hand, squeezing gently in support.

"I think I know," Diana stepped closer. "This is my grandmother," Diana explained. "She had two children. A boy and a girl. My mother and…according to what she just said…your father. Though both died in that car accident, and that was in Kansas. We lived there until recently. We moved here because of the climate and I think because Uncle Gus traveled here a lot on business and always talked about how much he loved Phoenix."

Tina smiled. "Maybe it wasn't the town he loved so much as a girl who lived here. I bet your uncle was courting Lance's mom."

Diana shrugged her shoulders and her eyes widened in wonder. "Stranger things have happened, I suppose. I think you're probably my cousin," Diana said, knowing her life was changing even more with every passing second. "And my Oma is probably your Oma too," she concluded with a tearful chuckle.

"What does oma mean?" Lance seemed thunderstruck and Diana didn't blame him.

"It's Dutch for grandma," she told him, well aware of the room full of wolf shapeshifters hanging on every word.

There was a feeling of rightness about this. A feeling of fulfillment. The wolves felt it too, and their hushed attention had a sort of reverence about it. Only the beat of the music in the next room went on in the background, but it didn't detract from the significance of the moment. Someone had thoughtfully closed the door to block out most of the sound.

"This is kind of hard to believe," Lance said finally, looking as if he wanted to just accept, but was too world-weary to take anything at face value.

"It's okay," Oma said quietly, her eyes shining. "We have time to look through the records and to show you images of Gustav. You look just like him at that age, you know." Oma paused to wipe at her cheeks, but her expression was joyous. "And there are many things we can share with you about the history of our people." Diana noticed her grandmother didn't mention the chronicles by name, but Diana knew that's what she meant.

"Why don't we all sit down," Diana put in, unable to break the habit of looking after her grandmother.

But Oma had all sorts of new strength and she led the way to a nearby table that was mostly empty and claimed it. She directed Tina and Lance to sit next to her with Diana and Adam on her other side.

Zeke was kind enough to get refreshments brought over to them as he joined the table without being asked. He seemed somewhat possessive of Diana's granny, which was kind of cute.

Oma reached out and put her aged hand over the back of Lance's where he'd rested it on the table. She paused a moment as their energies met for the first time, and then she smiled beatifically.

"You are my Gustav's son, though I know it will take a while for you to accept it. It doesn't matter. You are a firebird and my granddaughter has blessed me with the second of the firebird's magical gifts. I have long foreseen my own death, and it wasn't too far away." Here, she looked at Diana, who gasped, and smiled reassuringly. "But after today, everything changed. When Diana embraced the firebird fully, the gift sparked to life in her, and in me."

"What are these gifts you speak of?" Tina asked from beside Lance. She looked intrigued.

"It has been handed down in our family that there are several gifts the firebird can bestow. The first is being able to see and destroy evil. The second is longevity. The third, and rarest, is clairvoyance. I've always had a bit of the third. It seems Diana's transformation has gifted me with some of the second."

"And I have the first," Lance confirmed, nodding. "I've already done battle in my other form and I can both see evil and destroy it."

Diana nodded. Adam had said as much. But Oma's claim to have foreseen her own death still bothered Diana.

"Why didn't you warn me that you'd seen your end?" Diana asked her grandmother gently.

"I don't like to worry you, pumpkin," she said gently. "And besides… It's all changed. This evening I saw a new vision. Not my death. My future. And it was a long and happy one." Here, Oma surprised Diana by looking over at Zeke, who had sat across the table from Oma, smiling.

"You're not going to turn into a firebird too, are you?" Diana asked, half-amazed and half-appalled at the very thought of her ninety-something-year-old grandmother shapeshifting and flying all over the place. Could that even work?

Oma laughed hard at that. "Oh, no. It's too late for me, though I will reap the benefits of being in your family, now that you have transitioned. I'm going to live a lot longer than I would have otherwise. As will you, and everyone you love." Oma's voice was gentle with wonder.

"Barring crazy people coming after you and trying to steal your power," Tina put in, her tone cautionary.

"Has that happened?" Diana asked, concerned.

"Yes, unfortunately," Lance told her. "But we fought them off and the phoenix magic ended the threat."

"At least from that quarter," Tina added, darkly. "There are forces out there that would try to trap and kill you for your power. It's a great temptation to folks who like to take shortcuts on their way to the top. You'll have to be cautious, but with Stone at your side, you'll be a lot safer than you were before."

Adam put his arm around Diana's

shoulders and she immediately felt better. It shook her that there might be unknown danger gunning for her now that she'd transitioned, but as her grandmother had said... Things had changed. A lot. For all of them.

There were still a lot of details to work out, but Diana felt very positive about the future for her...with her mate.

EPILOGUE

The party lasted long into the night and Lance and Tina stayed 'til the end. Diana was glad. Oma seemed to enjoy just looking at Lance, which probably made the man a little uncomfortable, but he was a good sport about it. Diana realized at some point that she'd been given several amazing gifts. A mate to love and share her life with. A Pack that would be her new family. Actual blood-related family that she'd never known existed in Lance, and a promising new friend in

Tina. More time with her beloved grandmother, who looked better than Diana had seen her in years.

It was all almost too much. She sat back and watched the party, Adam at her side. Oma was happy. Lance looked thunderstruck. Tina was smiling at both of them with a sappy expression. And Zeke was so solicitous of Oma it was touching.

"Penny for your thoughts," Adam whispered near her ear, his arm around her shoulders tugging her close.

She turned in her seat to meet his gaze. "So much has happened in such a short time. It's a bit overwhelming, but it's all so *good*. It's like the Goddess decided to just shower us all with gifts all at once."

"You believe in the Mother of All?" Adam asked, seeming surprised.

"I was raised on the tales of the firebird in my own family. Of course we follow the old ways," she said, rolling her eyes. "We just don't talk about it in public, but I figured you were already in on the whole magical secret, right? Oma always said shifters followed the Goddess, too."

"Yeah, we do," he agreed. "I was just surprised. You were so...*human*, just

218

yesterday." He laughed and she joined in.

"What can I say? You bring out the best in me." She moved closer to give him a quick kiss on the lips.

"No, my love," he whispered back, keeping her close. "You do that for me. And for always."

Their kiss was a bit more involved this time and only ended when just about everyone in the room started howling and cheering. Life in the midst of a werewolf Pack was going to be interesting, but Diana was looking forward to getting used to it. These people were fun and fierce, and knew how to party. And her new mate was the man of her dreams in every respect.

Diana sent a silent prayer of thanks up to the Mother of All, knowing she'd been truly blessed.

*

In the town of Grizzly Cove, on the coast of Washington State, a dragon stirred. Something was going on to the south. Something very odd, indeed. Something he needed to investigate…

# # #

ABOUT THE AUTHOR

Bianca D'Arc has run a laboratory, climbed the corporate ladder in the shark-infested streets of lower Manhattan, studied and taught martial arts, and earned the right to put a whole bunch of letters after her name, but she's always enjoyed writing more than any of her other pursuits. She grew up and still lives on Long Island, where she keeps busy with an extensive garden, several aquariums full of very demanding fish, and writing her favorite genres of paranormal, fantasy and sci-fi romance.

Bianca loves to hear from readers and can be reached through Twitter (@BiancaDArc), Facebook (BiancaDArcAuthor) or through the various links on her website.

WELCOME TO THE D'ARC SIDE…
WWW.BIANCADARC.COM

OTHER BOOKS
BY BIANCA D'ARC

Paranormal Romance

Brotherhood of Blood
One & Only
Rare Vintage
Phantom Desires
Sweeter Than Wine
Forever Valentine
Wolf Hills*
Wolf Quest

Tales of the Were
Lords of the Were
Inferno
Rocky
Slade

Tales of the Were ~ Redstone Clan
The Purrfect Stranger
Grif
Red
Magnus
Bobcat
Matt

Dragon Knights ~ Sons of Draconia
FireDrake
Dragon Storm
Keeper of the Flame
Hidden Dragons

Dragon Knights ~ The Sea Captain's Daughter
Sea Dragon
Dragon Fire
Dragon Mates

Science Fiction Romance

StarLords
Hidden Talent
Talent For Trouble
Shy Talent

Jit'Suku Chronicles ~ Arcana
King of Swords
King of Cups
King of Clubs
King of Stars
End of the Line
Diva

Jit'Suku Chronicles ~ Sons of Amber
Angel in the Badlands
Master of Her Heart

Jit'Suku Chronicles ~ In the Stars
The Cyborg Next Door

Futuristic Erotic Romance

Resonance Mates
Hara's Legacy**
Davin's Quest
Jaci's Experiment
Grady's Awakening
Harry's Sacrifice

* RT Book Reviews Awards Nominee
** EPPIE Award Winner
*** CAPA Award Winner

WWW.BIANCADARC.COM

.

Made in the USA
Lexington, KY
19 August 2018